The New York Times

IN THE HEADLINES

Seeking Asylum

THE HUMAN COST

THE NEW YORK TIMES EDITORIAL STAFF

Published in 2021 by New York Times Educational Publishing
in association with The Rosen Publishing Group, Inc.
29 East 21st Street, New York, NY 10010

First Edition

The New York Times
Caroline Que: Editorial Director, Book Development
Cecilia Bohan: Photo Rights/Permissions Editor
Heidi Giovine: Administrative Manager

Rosen Publishing
Megan Kellerman: Managing Editor
Julia Bosson: Editor
Brian Garvey: Art Director

Cataloging-in-Publication Data
Names: New York Times Company.
Title: Seeking asylum: the human cost / edited by the New York
Times editorial staff.
Description: New York : New York Times Educational Publishing,
2021. | Series: In the headlines | Includes glossary and index.
Identifiers: ISBN 9781642824186 (library bound) | ISBN
9781642824179 (pbk.) | ISBN 9781642824193 (ebook)
Subjects: LCSH: Refugees—United States. | Refugees—United
States—Social conditions. | Asylum, Right of—United States.
Classification: LCC JV6601.S665 2021 | DDC 323.631—dc23

Manufactured in the United States of America

On the cover: Migrants from Guatemala walk along the Mexican
side of the border, looking for an opportunity to enter the United
States to seek asylum, in El Paso, Tex., on June 28, 2019; Ilana
Panich-Linsman for The New York Times.

Contents

CHAPTER 3

Life on the Border

CHAPTER 4

Life or Death

Perspectives on Asylum

Introduction

IN JUNE 2019, a photographer took an image of the bodies of a Salvadoran man, Óscar Alberto Martínez Ramírez, and his twenty-three-month-old daughter, who had drowned trying to cross the Rio Grande into Texas. The gruesome photograph added fuel to a debate that has been increasing in intensity during the Trump administration: As record numbers of Central American men, women and children have been driven to seek refuge inside the United States, the path to asylum has become more narrow and perilous, leading to a humanitarian crisis on American borders.

The number of asylum seekers has only increased over the past several years: In the first half of 2019, more than 350,000 men, women and children from El Salvador, Guatemala and Honduras had been picked up by U.S. Border Patrol. There are as many stories of harrowing journeys as there are individuals seeking safety, but the contours of many stay the same: There are men who have refused to cooperate with drug cartels, families fleeing the wrath of violent gangs, and individuals hunting for refuge on the basis of being members of religious or L.G.B.T. minority groups.

Under standard U.S. policy, once individuals have made it into America, asylum seekers are granted temporary residential status as they enter a highly complex legal process that, with a backlog of several hundred thousand cases, can take years to be settled one way or another. They work with judges, advocates, social workers and lawyers in order to have their story heard and tried. In order to pass muster, their reasons for seeking asylum must fit a highly specific set of criteria: Even the slightest variation can cause an otherwise unimpeachable case to be rejected.

Asylum seeker Selvin Alvarado, 29, with his son at a shelter in the border city of Tijuana, Mexico, March 22, 2019. Alvarado says he is considering sneaking into the United States if his asylum claim is further delayed.

The asylum system has been under stress for more than a decade, but it saw new levels of challenge with the ascendancy of Donald J. Trump. Trump's 2016 presidential platform was largely centered around increasing border security and tightening asylum laws. And in the early years of his administration, he made good on his promise to restrict access to America's heartland. His Departments of Justice and Homeland Security have restricted American asylum policy, narrowing both what can be considered grounds for asylum as well as complicating the steps necessary to receive asylum in the United States.

One strategy this administration has taken is the unprecedented act of preventing asylum seekers from entering the United States in the first place. In a law passed in 2019, the Trump administration ruled that individuals on their way to the United States must seek asylum in the first country they enter, meaning that most Central Americans who attempt to reach the United States through Mexico are legally required to request refuge there. Later the same year, Trump reached asylum deals with El Salvador and Guatemala, sending asylum seekers to await legal processes there.

For all intents and purposes, the United States–Mexico border has become closed to those who seek support and refuge in the United States, resulting in massive systems of poorly regulated camps and detention facilities. On the Mexican side, men, women and children wait with little sense of any political recourse and, increasingly, hope, vulnerable to the forces of traffickers and gang members who have made a habit of kidnapping asylum seekers for ransom. On the American side, families are experiencing the impact of Trump's family separation policy, which has resulted in detention facilities full of children without adequate food, protection or resources. The asylum process in the United States has become a compounded humanitarian crisis, exposing families who have already escaped the worst to further forms of danger and cruelty. If asylum means safety, then that is not what seekers will encounter. Instead, they find a system badly in need of reform.

CHAPTER 1

Understanding Asylum Policy

U.S. asylum policy changed drastically in the late 20th century. As political conflicts escalated in Central and South American countries, waves of asylum seekers appeared at the southern border, hoping for refuge. The United States has subsequently struggled to adjust, both adapting policy to offer more immediate help as well as narrowing the conditions for asylum when the sheer number of individuals increased dramatically.

In a Shift, U.S. Grants Asylum for Mexicans

BY SAM HOWE VERHOVEK | DEC. 1, 1995

HOUSTON, NOV. 30 — The United States has quietly granted political asylum to at least 55 Mexican citizens in the last 14 months, a major shift after many years in which virtually all asylum applications from Mexicans were routinely rejected.

Immigrants-rights advocates hail these grants of asylum, which are made by individual Federal immigration agents and judges on a case-by-case basis, as a collective milestone that amounts to formal recognition by the United States that political repression occurs in Mexico. But the actions have created a growing diplomatic headache for the Clinton Administration by angering the Mexican Government and the ruling party that has dominated the country for more than 60 years.

The asylum approvals come during a time of huge increases in the numbers of such applications from Mexicans. Applications increased to 9,304 in the 1995 fiscal year, which ended Sept. 30, from 6,397 in 1993 and from only 122 in 1990. From 1990 through 1993, not a single asylum application was approved; in 1994 five were approved, and in the most recent fiscal year it was 54.

The cause of the increase is itself the subject of intense debate. Advocates for those seeking asylum say the increase reflects the Mexican public's growing opposition to the ruling political party and asylum applicants' fears of retaliation for their political activities. But Federal immigration officials say that much of the increase represents fraudulent applications submitted by Mexicans seeking to take advantage of a loophole in the asylum law that allowed them to work legally in the United States pending review of an asylum request.

Among those granted asylum are environmentalists and critics of the Government, including the former Mayor of Ojinaga, Ernesto Poblano, and Ana Maria Guillen, the former leader of the opposition Democratic Revolutionary Party in Matamoros, near the United States border.

"I'm happy because we have created an opening for our compatriots," said Ms. Guillen, whose petition was approved this week by an immigration judge in San Antonio. "I'm sad because the situation is worse and we don't have the conditions that will allow us to return."

A portrait of these refugees is difficult to assemble: the Federal Immigration and Naturalization Service, citing confidentiality laws, declined to release details of the asylum petitions that have been approved.

In the vast majority of cases, asylum requests from Mexico are still turned down, a point that both Mexican and State Department officials emphasized in interviews. And Gustavo Mohar, the minister in charge of immigration affairs at the Mexican Embassy in Washington, insisted Mexican citizens had no reason to fear retribution for their political activities.

"We have in Mexico the mechanisms to protect people who feel their life is threatened," Mr. Mohar said today in a telephone interview. "The Government position is that there is no action against people. They can speak and say whatever they will."

The Immigration and Naturalization Service has taken pains to portray the surge in asylum petitions as largely the result of fraudulent claims. But even after the provision that allowed applicants to begin working legally was rescinded early this year under a much-heralded reform of asylum procedures, the numbers of applications increased slightly over the year before.

And advocates for the Mexican petitioners say a growing number of opposition leaders in Mexico have cited abuse, torture and fear for their lives in their requests to remain in the United States — and several have persuaded immigration judges to approve their requests based on such evidence.

"There is this sort of myth that Mexico is functioning as a full democracy where people can object without facing reprisals," said Dan Kesselbrenner, director of the immigration project of the National Lawyers Guild, a resource center for groups that represent immigrants.

"The willingness of judges to grant asylum relief to people from Mexico reflects the actual objective conditions in Mexico," he said, "where there is political repression of people who are active against the Government."

And Maria Jimenez, director of the immigration law-enforcement monitoring project of the American Friends Service Committee here in Houston, said the rulings "corroborate what Amnesty International and Americas Watch have reported, that there's no prosecution of people, the police or army or anyone, who commits these violations."

Under Federal immigration statutes, asylum is approved if an applicant can demonstrate "a well-founded fear of persecution based on race, religion, nationality, political opinion or membership in a particular social group." The approval can come from officers of the naturalization service or Federal immigration judges.

In one case last year, in apparently the first specific ruling by immigration authorities that sexual orientation constituted grounds for persecution, a gay Mexican man was granted asylum after contending he was harassed, tortured and raped by Mexican police.

Most of the Mexican cases appear to involve political activism. Carlos Spector Calderon, an El Paso lawyer, said he had represented or advised five people granted asylum in the past few years, all of whom held leadership positions in opposition parties.

Still, some of those granted asylum have apparently not applied on political grounds. For instance, an official familiar with immigration rulings said today that among those granted asylum last year were several relatives of a man accused in the assassination of the Mexican Presidential candidate, Luis Donaldo Colosio.

The relatives were not themselves involved in political activities and simply feared retaliation, said the official, who spoke on condition of anonymity. But a spokesman for the immigration service said the agency could not confirm that account.

Ms. Guillen said Mexican officials had put out a warrant for her arrest after she was attacked by police when she tried to enter a building where ballots were being counted. She fled to San Antonio and at her hearing, presented testimony from Juan Gutierrez, a colleague who said he had been held by the police, beaten and threatened with "disappearance." She also presented affidavits from witnesses who said they had seen other members of the party beaten.

In a ruling on Monday, a Federal immigration judge, Richard F. Brodsky, said Ms. Guillen was "similarly situated" to members of her party who had been the subject of persecution, and he approved her request. In doing so, he overruled an earlier denial of the application by the immigration service.

Asked if she wanted to return to Mexico eventually, she said: "If the conditions allow, of course. I will return to my country when they get better."

Big Disparities in Judging of Asylum Cases

BY JULIA PRESTON | MAY 31, 2007

ASYLUM SEEKERS IN the United States face broad disparities in the nation's 54 immigration courts, with the outcome of cases influenced by things like the location of the court and the sex and professional background of judges, a new study has found.

The study, by three law professors, analyzes 140,000 decisions by immigration judges, including those cases from the 15 countries that have produced the most asylum seekers in recent years, among them China, Haiti, Colombia, Albania and Russia. The professors compared for the first time the results of immigration court cases over more than four years, finding vast differences in the handling of claims with generally comparable factual circumstances.

In one of the starker examples cited, Colombians had an 88 percent chance of winning asylum from one judge in the Miami immigration court and a 5 percent chance from another judge in the same court.

"It is very disturbing that these decisions can mean life or death, and they seem to a large extent to be the result of a clerk's random assignment of a case to a particular judge," said an author of the study, Philip G. Schrag, a professor at Georgetown University Law Center.

The study offers an unusually detailed window into the overburdened and often erratic immigration courts. Though the immigration bill now being considered does not propose major revisions in asylum laws, those courts serve as the judicial backbone of the immigration system that would take on an immense new workload if the bill becomes law.

The legislation would offer a road to legal status to an estimated 12 million illegal immigrants, eliminate backlogs of legal immigration cases and step up enforcement, among other measures. Experts predict countless legal snags that would land before the immigration judges.

Officials at the Executive Office for Immigration Review of the Department of Justice, which oversees the immigration courts, declined to allow interviews about the study with David L. Neal, the chief immigration judge, citing a policy that immigration judges do not speak with the news media about their rulings.

The study found that someone who has fled China in fear of persecution and asks for asylum in immigration court in Orlando, Fla., has an excellent — 76 percent — chance of success, while the same refugee would have a 7 percent chance in Atlanta. Similarly, a Haitian seeking refuge from political violence is almost twice as likely to succeed in New York as in Miami.

Immigration lawyers acknowledge that the judges have difficult work, with huge dockets of cases that must be decided speedily on the basis of scant or subjective information. Often the asylum seeker is the only witness to crucial events.

But because immigration law is federal, the study's authors argued, some uniformity could be expected in judges' asylum rulings across the country, particularly in cases of people fleeing a country, like China or Colombia, where the conditions of political oppression or civil violence are publicly known.

"It's such a high-volume system where the participants have so little time to test cases and make decisions, you become much more subject to the general viewpoint of the judge," said Bo Cooper, a lawyer at Paul, Hastings, Janofsky & Walker who is a former general counsel of the Immigration and Naturalization Service. That has created a risk, Mr. Cooper said, that "the system will not be good enough at providing refuge to those in need or identifying the claims of those who are not in need."

The wide discretion exercised by immigration judges can be disheartening to lawyers and disastrous for immigrants facing threats to their lives if they are forced to return home, immigration lawyers said.

"Oftentimes, it's just the luck of the draw," said Cheryl Little, a lawyer and executive director of the Florida Immigrant Advocacy

Center, a legal assistance group in Miami that represents many asylum seekers. "It's heartbreaking," Ms. Little said. "How do you explain to people asking for refuge that even in the United States of America we can't assure them they will receive due process and justice?"

While immigration officers at Citizenship and Immigration Services, the federal agency, can grant asylum, the majority of asylum cases are decided by the immigration judges. Under the immigration system, refugees are foreigners coming from abroad who win residency in the United States for protection from religious persecution or political threats. Asylum is granted to foreigners who apply for refuge when they are already in the United States.

The study is based on data on judges' decisions from January 2000 through August 2004. It will be posted today on the Web site of the Social Science Research Network, www.ssrn.com, and published in November in the Stanford Law Review.

In addition to Professor Schrag, the authors are Andrew I. Schoenholtz, also a professor at Georgetown University Law Center, and Jaya Ramji-Nogales, a professor at Beasley School of Law at Temple University.

According to the study, great differences also prevail among judges sitting on the same court and hearing similar asylum cases. In the Miami immigration court, one judge granted 3 percent of the asylum cases, while another granted 75 percent.

One of the most significant factors determining whether a judge would be likely to approve asylum petitions was sex, the study found. Female immigration judges grant asylum at a 44 percent higher rate than their male colleagues.

The study by the three professors did not examine the judges' political affiliation or the administration that appointed them.

The study suggests that the different willingness to grant asylum between male and female judges may in part have to do with their backgrounds. Of 78 female judges in the study, 27 percent had previously worked for organizations that defended the rights of immigrants or the poor, while only 8 percent of 169 male judges had similar experience.

Though the study does not identify judges by name, profiles of immigration judges were drawn up separately by the Transactional Records Access Clearinghouse, a research group at Syracuse University. They show that the 24 judges who sit today in Miami (21 in court and 3 based in a detention facility) include some of the most likely and least likely to grant asylum.

According to the Clearinghouse profiles, one immigration judge currently on the Miami court, Mahlon F. Hanson, granted 3 percent of the asylum cases he heard. He was the second-toughest judge in the nation on asylum issues, the group found. Judge Denise N. Slavin, who hears cases at the Krome North detention center in Miami, granted 59 percent of the asylum claims she considered, placing her in the top 15 percent of judges approving such claims.

Lawyers said the variations may in part have to do with the cases particular courts are handling. Miami immigration courts see a large number of asylum claims from Haiti, and the judges may have differing outlooks and disagree about the possibilities for Haitians to face persecution in their country.

The variations between courts and among judges were particularly troubling, the authors of the study argued, because of the impact of procedural changes introduced by the Bush administration in 2002 at the Board of Immigration Appeals, the appellate body that reviews decisions by the immigration court judges.

Those changes led to a "sudden and lasting decline" in appeals that were favorable to asylum seekers, the study found, raising doubts as to whether the board was providing fair appeals.

In 2002, Attorney General John Ashcroft made streamlined the work of the appeals board, reducing the number of board members to 11 from 23 and encouraging more decisions by single members and without explanation.

The study looked at 76,000 decisions by the appeals board from 1998 through 2005. Asylum applicants who were represented by lawyers received favorable appeals decisions from the board in 43 percent of cases in 2001, the year before the changes took effect. By 2005, asylum seekers with lawyers won their appeals in 13 percent of cases.

"The judges handle a very large caseload, they're human, they are not going to catch every detail," said Mary Meg McCarthy, director of the National Immigrant Justice Center, a legal assistance group in Chicago. "But once they streamlined the Board of Immigration Appeals," Ms. McCarthy said, "there was a failure of the board to review those cases, to check on what the immigration judge had found. When that failed, we had a real crisis in the system."

As a result of the trends at the appeals board, there has been a new surge of asylum appeals to the federal circuit courts, in practice the last resort for immigration cases. Over all, the number of people winning asylum in the United States has declined, dropping by about 12 percent from 28,684 in 2003 to 25,257 in 2005, the last year when complete figures are available.

The immigration courts have been in the spotlight after Justice Department officials said last week that the investigation of Monica M. Goodling, a former aide to Attorney General Alberto R. Gonzales, has been expanded to include her role in helping to appoint immigration judges.

Ms. Goodling testified last week that she had "crossed the line" in applying political considerations to candidates for nonpartisan legal jobs. Immigration judges are appointed by the attorney general, and 49 of 226 current judges were appointed during the tenure of Mr. Gonzales.

New Policy Permits Asylum for Battered Women

BY JULIA PRESTON | JULY 15, 2009

THE OBAMA ADMINISTRATION has opened the way for foreign women who are victims of severe domestic beatings and sexual abuse to receive asylum in the United States. The action reverses a Bush administration stance in a protracted and passionate legal battle over the possibilities for battered women to become refugees.

In addition to meeting other strict conditions for asylum, abused women will need to show that they are treated by their abuser as subordinates and little better than property, according to an immigration court filing by the administration, and that domestic abuse is widely tolerated in their country. They must show that they could not find protection from institutions at home or by moving to another place within their own country.

The administration laid out its position in an immigration appeals court filing in the case of a woman from Mexico who requested asylum, saying she feared she would be murdered by her common-law husband there. According to court documents filed in San Francisco, the man repeatedly raped her at gunpoint, held her captive, stole from her and at one point tried to burn her alive when he learned she was pregnant.

The government submitted its legal brief in April, but the woman only recently gave her consent for the confidential case documents to be disclosed to The New York Times. The government has marked a clear, although narrow, pathway for battered women seeking asylum, lawyers said, after 13 years of tangled court arguments, including resistance from the Bush administration to recognize any of those claims.

Moving cautiously, the Department of Homeland Security did not immediately recommend asylum for the Mexican woman, who is identified in the court papers only by her initials as L.R. But the department, in the unusual submission written by senior government lawyers, concluded in plain terms that "it is possible" that the Mexican woman "and other applicants who have experienced domestic violence could qualify for asylum."

As recently as last year, Bush administration lawyers had argued in the same case that in spite of her husband's brutality, L.R. and other battered women could not meet the standards of American asylum law.

"This really opens the door to the protection of women who have suffered these kinds of violations," said Karen Musalo, a professor who is director of the Center for Gender and Refugee Studies at the University of California Hastings College of the Law in San Francisco. Professor Musalo has represented other abused women seeking asylum and recently took up the case of L.R.

The Obama administration's position caps a legal odyssey for foreign women seeking protection in the United States from domestic abuse that began in 1996 when a Guatemalan woman named Rody Alvarado was granted asylum by an immigration court, based on her account of repeated beatings by her husband. Three years later, an immigration appeals court overturned Ms. Alvarado's asylum, saying she was not part of any persecuted group under American law.

Since then Ms. Alvarado's case has stalled as successive administrations debated the issue, with immigration officials reluctant to open a floodgate of asylum petitions from battered women across the globe. During the Clinton administration, Attorney General Janet Reno proposed regulations to clarify the matter, but they have never gone into effect. In a briefing paper in 2004, lawyers for the Department of Homeland Security raised the possibility of asylum for victims of domestic violence, but the Bush administration never put that into practice in immigration court, Professor Musalo said.

Now Homeland Security officials say they are returning to views the department put forward in 2004, refining them to draw conditions sufficiently narrow that battered women would prevail in only a limited number cases.

"Although each case is highly fact-dependent and requires scrutiny of the specific threat an applicant faces," said Matt Chandler, a spokesman for the Department of Homeland Security, "the department continues to view domestic violence as a possible basis for asylum in the United States." He said officials hoped to complete regulations governing the complex cases.

The new policy does not involve women fleeing genital mutilation.

Any applicant for asylum or refugee status in the United States must demonstrate a "well-founded fear of persecution" because of race, religion, nationality, political opinion or "membership in a particular social group." The extended legal argument has been whether abused women could be part of any social group that would be eligible under those terms. Last year, 22,930 people won asylum in this country fleeing all types of persecution; the number has been decreasing in recent years.

Because asylum cases are confidential, there is no way of knowing how many applications by battered women have been denied or held up over the last decade. The issue is further complicated by the peculiarities of the United States immigration system, in which asylum cases are heard in courts that are not part of the federal judiciary, but are run by an agency of the Justice Department, with Homeland Security officials representing the government.

The government has not disputed the painful history that L.R., now 42, recounts in a court declaration. The man who became her tormentor first assaulted her when she was a teenager and he was a physical education coach, 14 years her senior, at a high school in the Mexican state of Guanajuato. He and his family were regarded as wealthy and influential because they owned a restaurant in town, L.R. said.

Over the years, he made her live with him, and forced her to have sex with him by putting a gun or a machete to her head, by breaking her nose and by threatening to kill the small children of her sister. Once when she became pregnant, she said, she barely escaped alive after he had poured kerosene on the bed where she was sleeping and ignited it. He stole the salary she earned as a teacher and later sold her teacher's license.

Local police dismissed her reports of violence as "a private matter," the court documents said, and a judge she turned to for help tried to seduce her.

"In Mexico, men believe they have a right to abuse their women because they are like a possession," she said. With three children born from her involuntary sex with the man, who never married her, she fled to California in 2004.

An immigration judge denied her asylum claim in 2006. In its new filing, the government urged that L.R.'s case be sent back to the immigration court for further review, suggesting she might still succeed. But the government also injected a caveat, insisting that "this does not mean that every victim of domestic violence would be eligible for asylum."

Who Qualifies for 'Asylum'?

ESSAY | BY EMILY BAZELON | SEPT. 15, 2015

IT'S AN ANCIENT PROMISE: When outsiders flee to a new place in desperate need, they will not be turned away. The Hebrew Bible speaks of six cities of refuge where someone who caused a death unwittingly would be protected from being killed in revenge. The Greeks allowed slaves who ran away from abusive masters and even some criminals to seek sanctuary in certain temples; "asylum" comes from their word for inviolable. According to legend, Romulus, the founder of Rome, extended asylum to people we would call migrants, choosing a spot between two groves on Capitoline Hill for his city's temple of asylum. "A crowd of commoners, both free and enslaved, poured in from the neighboring territories, eager for new conditions," the historian Livy wrote. "This was the first step towards the strength Romulus envisioned for Rome."

The right of asylum might seem as culturally embedded as the ruins of one of the old temples. According to international law, if a person merits asylum by showing she has a "well-founded fear of being persecuted" based on race, nationality, religion, political opinion or membership in a particular social group, she is no longer a migrant, who can be sent away at any time. She must be recognized as a refugee, with a right to be protected for as long as it is unsafe to return home. Yet many of the 380,000 people who have arrived in Europe this year from countries like Syria, Eritrea and Afghanistan have sought legal refuge, risking suffocation in smugglers' trucks and drowning at sea, only to find themselves described as a threat and a nuisance.

Prime Minister David Cameron of Britain invoked insects when he warned of a "swarm" of "illegal migrants." Prime Minister Victor Orbán of Hungary is throwing up a fence along his country's southern border with Serbia and refusing to register asylum claims. "From a European perspective, the number of potential future immigrants seems limitless," he warned, making the disorder he helped create sound intractable. Most of those arriving, he emphasized, "are not Christians, but Muslims," adding, "Europe is not in the grip of a 'refugee problem' or a 'refugee situation,' but the European Continent is threatened by an ever-mounting wave of modern-era migration." In other words, in his view, the people arriving in Hungary are not entitled to protection.

The modern right to asylum has roots in the aftermath of World War I and the Russian Revolution. Fleeing famine and the Bolsheviks, an unprecedented wave of 1.5 million Russians streamed into Europe. They had been stripped of citizenship by the Soviet government, and their plight gave rise to terms that reflected their statelessness. In 1921, the nascent Council of the League of Nations authorized "certificates of identity" for all "Russian refugees." More than 50 countries agreed to recognize the documents, which gave the Russians the right to work and resettle.

The system began to crack, however, as Nazi aggression destabilized the Continent. In the 1930s, few countries signed the accords that would have provided asylum to Germans, Austrians and Czechs escaping the Nazis. The St. Louis, a ship filled with more than 900 Jews, symbolized the failure of the era: Denied entry by Cuba, the United States and Canada in 1939, it was forced to return to Europe on the eve of the Holocaust. After the war, the international community tried to make amends. A landmark treaty, the 1951 Refugee Convention, expressed "profound concern" for refugees and established the standard for attaining asylum that remains in place today. From this era comes the forlorn, perhaps romantic memory of the post-World War II refugee, worthy of more sympathy than a migrant (an ostensibly neutral word now tainted by its proximity to "illegal immigrant").

But even in that moment of accord, there was still a question of who would bear responsibility for the flood of bodies with their urgent needs. "The grant of asylum may place unduly heavy burdens on certain countries," the treaty's preamble stated, such that global protection cannot be achieved "without international cooperation." Today, while Europe squabbles over quotas, 86 percent of the world's 19 million refugees live in developing countries like Ethiopia, Kenya and Pakistan. Turkey has more than two million Syrian asylum-seekers — compared with zero for the wealthy countries of the Persian Gulf. There has been far more global fractiousness than collaboration, though Chancellor Angela Merkel of Germany, preparing her country to accept 800,000 people this year, reminded the world that the international right to asylum "has no limits on the number of asylum-seekers."

The United States prides itself on having accepted 70,000 new refugees last year. But the battle over who counts as a migrant and who counts as a refugee plays out over and over again on the Southern border. Last summer, when tens of thousands of children from Central America tried to enter the United States, some were turned away, and others were held in bleak border camps. One big fight is over whether a child or a teenager can win asylum because of his fear of being a target of gang recruiting or violence related to the drug wars. So far, the answer has frequently been no. That is the backdrop for a proposal by Secretary of State John Kerry to increase the total number of refugees we accept to 100,000 in 2016. President Obama said this number should include 10,000 Syrians. These proposals are modest at best, and they barely address this crisis, much less the next one.

Twenty years ago, a team of lawyers, social scientists, government officials and activists led by James C. Hathaway, now a law professor at the University of Michigan, gathered to brainstorm ideas to address the problem of sheltering and resettling large numbers of people. First, they proposed separating the determination of who merits asylum from the decision about where they go. Once a person is designated a refugee, he or she would receive entry to some safe harbor in the world, based on a set of quotas agreed upon by participating countries in advance. Syrians seeking refugee status who cross the border into Lebanon would receive the same treatment as those who make the perilous sea journey to Greece or Italy.

The record of the past few decades shows that within five to seven years of the kind of war or upheaval that prompts mass flight, conflict often abates, and about half of the refugees then choose to go home. For those who cannot safely return, Hathaway's model provides for the possibility that another host country could take over from the first, in hopes of increasing shared responsibility. Last year, only about 100,000 refugees across the globe received permanent resettlement status. A more orderly — and shared — system could benefit the millions who now live in limbo.

This may seem like a fantasy given the current turmoil. And yet the world has come together to solve a refugee crisis before. In the decade after the Vietnam War, millions of Vietnamese fled their country, often by sea. Nicknamed the "boat people," they landed throughout Southeast Asia, where governments eventually threatened to stop accepting them. After an international conference in 1979, those countries dropped their threat, and the rest of the world, especially nations in the West, agreed to take on the task of permanent resettlement and pay most of the cost. Over a decade or so, about 1.8 million Vietnamese refugees were resettled, blending into the human crowd, living out their lives in new lands.

EMILY BAZELON is a staff writer for the magazine.

Trump and the Battle Over Sanctuary in America

RETRO REPORT | BY CLYDE HABERMAN | MARCH 5, 2017

Retro Report re-examines the leading stories of decades past through essays and video documentaries.

THE CONCEPT OF sanctuary cities is deeply embedded in Western tradition. In biblical times, shelter was offered even to those who might have qualified as "bad hombres" in the eyes of President Trump. Killers, for example. If the crime lacked intent, they could flee to havens specifically designated in Deuteronomy and the Book of Joshua.

Skip ahead 3,500 years or so and societally sanctioned refuge is proving as powerful a concern for Americans today as it was for the ancients. Sanctuary cities — and counties and states — loom large as Mr. Trump seeks to vastly expand and speed the deportation of undocumented immigrants while threatening to withhold federal money from localities that refuse to cooperate with immigration officials.

To switch the biblical reference point to Ecclesiastes, there is no new thing under the sun, certainly not in regard to sanctuary. Retro Report, essays and video documentaries examining major news stories of the past and their continued relevance, begins a new series by recalling the so-called sanctuary movement of the 1980s, which put church and state in conflict with each other over the fate of Central Americans fleeing civil wars and pleading for asylum in the United States. Those refugees found President Ronald Reagan's White House no more eager to open its arms than the Trump administration is now to embrace Syrians seeking shelter from carnage back home.

The Reagan administration supported military governments in El Salvador and Guatemala, viewing them as bulwarks against pro-Communist insurgencies. And so it played down widespread human rights outrages by those regimes and affiliated death squads. When Salvadorans and Guatemalans tried to enter the United States, claiming a fear of persecution in their homelands, they typically were labeled "economic migrants," not political refugees.

Few were granted asylum — less than 3 percent in 1984. By comparison, Poles fleeing Communism were 10 times as likely that year to find asylum here. Anti-ayatollah Iranians were 20 times as likely.

With the front door to the United States effectively shut, Central Americans turned to a back entrance. This was the sanctuary movement. In the 1980s, it came to be embraced by hundreds of churches and synagogues, as well as by some college campuses and cities, in more than 30 states. Refugees denied political asylum were spirited across the southern border and sheltered in houses of worship like Southside Presbyterian Church in Tucson.

"These were middle-class folks who were fleeing for their lives," the Rev. John M. Fife, Southside's pastor in the 1980s, said of one group of asylum seekers.

"We'd take in people who had torture marks all over their body, and the immigration judge would order them deported the next day," said Mr. Fife, who is retired. When it came to smuggling and hiding people, he said, "I assumed it was illegal, but I could not claim to be a Christian and not be involved in trying to protect refugees' lives."

In all, an estimated 2,000 refuge seekers were aided in that latter-day version of the Underground Railroad. Unavoidably, the clergy made itself a foe of the government, which argued that no one was above the law and that the sanctuary movement was, at heart, inspired more by politics than by theological imperatives. Movement members were put on trial. In one celebrated 1980s case, eight of them, including Mr. Fife, were convicted of felony conspiracy and other charges. None ended up going to jail, however.

"Sometimes," Mr. Fife said at the time, "you cannot love both God and the civil authority. Sometimes you have to make a choice."

The issue today for people who share his beliefs is not so much how to bring unauthorized immigrants into the United States as it is how to keep millions already here from being tossed out.

Dozens of cities and many times that number of counties describe themselves as sanctuaries. What that means in practice can be elusive. In some places, the police are ordered not to inquire about immigration status when they take people into custody. Some cities openly refuse to cooperate with federal requests to hold undocumented immigrants until they can be deported. Mayor Bill de Blasio of New York, a Democrat, pledged cooperation if public safety was threatened, but "what we will not do," he said, "is turn our N.Y.P.D. officers into immigration agents." Other cities call themselves sanctuaries but have no clearly articulated policy.

As far as Mr. Trump and many fellow Republicans are concerned, failing to deport unauthorized immigrants is to invite the "bad hombres" among them to commit crimes. In his address to Congress last week, the president singled out several murders ascribed to undocumented immigrants. Often cited by him is the 2015 murder of Kathryn Steinle, 32, who was shot as she strolled on a pier in San Francisco. The man charged with killing her was a Mexican laborer with a long criminal record who had been deported from the United States five times, yet somehow managed to keep coming back.

To sanctuary defenders, evocations of a case like the Steinle murder amount to setting policy by anecdote. Studies show that crime rates among unauthorized immigrants are lower than those among native-born Americans.

Moreover, some local officials say it is not their job to enforce federal law. Many of them argue that it is self-defeating for cities to make undocumented but otherwise law-abiding immigrants feel vulnerable and afraid of the authorities. "We have to have people that cooperate with their local police if we're going to have any effect at all on the crime rate," Sheriff John Urquhart of King County in Washington State told Retro Report.

Early in the Obama presidency, the government took a hard line. Immigrants without proper papers faced deportation for all manner of infractions, criminal and noncriminal alike. Expulsions reached record highs, at one point surpassing 400,000 a year.

But many Obama supporters felt that the policy was unduly harsh, and the administration came to agree. In its final years, it focused principally on people who were deemed threats to national security, were convicted of serious crimes or were recent border crossers. Even with those tighter standards, plenty of people were sent packing: more than 240,000 in 2016, according to the federal Immigration and Customs Enforcement. Mexicans, Guatemalans, Hondurans and Salvadorans accounted for 94 percent of the total.

Mr. Trump has proposed returning to a more aggressive approach: rounding up and expelling potentially millions of people, including those not convicted of serious wrongdoing or, for that matter, even charged with any crime at all other than being in the United States without legal blessing. But the president created some confusion about his intentions when he surprisingly suggested in a private meeting with television anchors last week that he was open to finding a way to let millions of the undocumented stay in the country legally. What he meant was hardly plain. Publicly, his hard line on illegal immigration remained intact.

To carry out mass deportations, thousands of new immigration and customs agents would be hired, and local police officers and sheriff's deputies would be recruited.

To do that, the president would need the cooperation of state, county and city officials. What if he does not get it? Mr. Trump has said he is prepared to cut off federal funds to those localities. It is not a threat they can take lightly. New York City, for one, relies on aid from Washington for about 10 percent of its $85 billion annual budget.

A sign of what could happen nationally emerged last month in Texas, where Gov. Greg Abbott canceled $1.5 million in criminal justice grants to Travis County, whose seat is Austin, the state capital. This was after the county sheriff renounced cooperation with immigration officials seeking deportations.

How far Mr. Trump intends to take his threat is unclear. Will all federal aid to sanctuary cities be imperiled or just certain programs? No doubt, any cutoff of funds would invite court fights that could take many months, or even years, to settle.

In the meantime, the sanctuary movement could still pack a punch. That was suggested by Elizabeth M. McCormick, who teaches immigration and asylum law at the University of Tulsa College of Law. "We're at a moment in history right now," she told Retro Report, "that may be similar to the 1980s, when individuals felt that they needed to stand up for what's right."

A Refugee Caravan Is Hoping for Asylum in the U.S. How Are These Cases Decided?

BY MIRIAM JORDAN | APRIL 30, 2018

RUSSIAN BALLET DANCERS, Cuban baseball players and Chinese political dissidents. These are the kind of people fleeing persecution in their homelands who typically won asylum in the United States over the years.

In many cases, they were in the country for a theatrical performance, a conference or a sports tournament, then sought refuge. Think Martina Navratilova, the Czech tennis player, who defected during the 1975 U.S. Open.

Over the past five years, though, the number of asylum applications has skyrocketed. Civil wars in Africa, gang violence in Central America and government crackdowns in China have contributed to a backlog of hundreds of thousands of cases and processing times of up to six years. This presents a range of challenges to U.S. authorities, who are required under international law to give all of the cases careful consideration.

This week, a caravan of 150 to 200 migrants, mainly from Honduras, Guatemala and El Salvador, is waiting at the Mexican border in Tijuana to claim asylum, hoping to win permission to stay in the United States. But President Trump has urged his administration to redouble its efforts to enforce border laws, referring to the caravan over the weekend as "that mess," and declaring, "We have the worst laws anywhere in the world, we don't have borders."

Here's a look at how we got here, and what America's legal obligations are.

WHAT IS THE LEGAL BACKDROP?

The international agreement to protect asylum seekers emerged after the horrific events of World War II. The United Nations signed the refugee convention in 1951, which the United States ratified and incorporated into law in 1980.

The goal is to provide a safe haven for those who can prove they are fleeing persecution in their homeland.

WHAT'S THE DIFFERENCE BETWEEN A REFUGEE AND AN ASYLUM-SEEKER?

There are two ways people can win protection and the right to live permanently in the United States. In both cases they must prove the same well-founded fear of persecution on account of race, religion, nationality, political opinion or membership in a particular social group.

People who apply and are selected overseas eventually enter the United States as refugees.

Many of them, hundreds of thousands, remain parked in camps as the refugee application process unfolds, typically over several years. That process involves several interviews with United Nations and American officials. The United States also conducts several layers of security screening.

People already on United States soil apply for asylum.

Alexander Godunov, a principal dancer with the renowned Bolshoi Ballet, was granted asylum in the United States in 1979. He was the first of several dancers to defect from the Bolshoi during that year's tour in the United States. He requested asylum in New York City and received it immediately. Ms. Navratilova received asylum in October 1975, a month after filing for it.

During the 1980s, civil war in El Salvador displaced several hundred thousand people. Tens of thousands flocked to the United States and applied for political asylum.

Nowadays, the process of applying for asylum often takes years to complete, from start to finish. It involves interviews with United States immigration officials and often with immigration judges.

Whether people entered the country legally or not, they are eligible to apply for asylum.

THE SURGE

The world is suffering the worst refugee crisis since World War II. There are now a staggering number of refugees, asylum-seekers and displaced people — about 50 million.

Violence around the globe is pushing desperate people to seek safety across international borders. People from the Middle East and Africa are taking rickety boats and making treacherous treks to reach Europe. They are less likely to show up at the southwest border of the United States than people from Latin America who are, relatively speaking, nearby and can come over land.

In recent years, violence in Central America — it has some of the highest murder rates in the world — has prompted tens of thousands of people since 2014 to make the perilous journey to the United States.

The migrants either turn themselves in at the border to American authorities or sneak into the country illegally. Regardless, they then declare that they are seeking asylum.

Before 2011, only 1 percent of all arriving foreigners requested asylum. Today, one out of 10 apply, according to government officials.

THE CARAVAN

Jeff Sessions, the United States Attorney General, called the caravan now awaiting processing at the San Ysidro port of entry a "deliberate attempt to undermine our laws and overwhelm our system."

"There is no right to demand entry without justification," he said, adding that he would deploy prosecutors to handle cases.

Indeed, there are signs that the administration is seeking to disqualify certain applicants, such as victims of domestic violence, who have sometimes won asylum. Recently, Mr. Sessions suggested they should not be eligible.

Yet the law does require authorities to accept and consider their petitions.

Once they are processed at the port of entry, they are likely to be transferred to a detention facility where they must pass the first step in the asylum process, a "credible-fear" interview with an officer of the United States Immigration and Citizenship Services.

The number of credible-fear interviews conducted by the federal agency has soared from 5,000 in 2007 to 80,000 last year.

More than three quarters of those interviewed pass that screening and are referred to an immigration judge for hearings that may span months or longer. (Those who fail the interview can be deported immediately.)

Asylum applicants awaiting a hearing before a judge either remain in detention or are released wearing a tracking device, such as an ankle monitor, with a date to appear in court.

Many Central Americans stay with friends and relatives who already live in the United States. Once 180 days have passed after filing of their application, they are eligible to work in the United States. Their children attend public schools.

Because some migrants in the past have skipped their court hearings, Mr. Trump has criticized the practice of releasing migrants, describing it as "catch and release." In recent months, his administration has ordered border officers to, when possible, keep these migrants in detention, rather than release them.

"While these asylum seekers are, on paper, eligible for consideration for release on parole, in reality ICE holds them in detention for long periods of time," said Eleanor Acer, director of refugee protection for Human Rights First.

United States officials say the administration is trying to figure out how to deal with the surge in asylum applications in a manner that is consistent with its international obligations.

Part of the problem is that immigration courts are clogged, and not just with asylum cases.

At of the end of March, there were 692,298 cases in the backlog, according to Syracuse University's Transactional Records Access Clearinghouse, which tracks the trends. The average wait time for current pending cases was 718 days, or nearly two years.

ARE THEIR CLAIMS LEGITIMATE?

Central Americans who apply for asylum often have been threatened with death or suffered attacks at the hands of gangs. Often mothers flee to protect their children from recruitment.

"We have seen firsthand the extraordinarily violent conditions in the Northern Triangle of Central America that forces families and children to flee their homes in search of urgently needed safety in the U.S.," said Jennifer Sime, senior vice president of United States programs at the International Rescue Committee.

"Those who qualify and are fleeing violence, who have no other route to protection, should be granted safety and asylum," she said.

Immigrant advocates say their circumstances are akin to those faced by people escaping war in Syria or Somalia. However, it is more difficult for Central Americans to win their cases.

"A huge percentage of these people get deported," said Marty Rosenbluth, an immigration attorney. "It's a really difficult struggle to win asylum."

Mr. Rosenbluth said that all of his asylum cases based on gang violence have failed because his clients could not establish that they fit into a social group suffering particular persecution to qualify.

In some cases, judges have found that applicants fabricated or exaggerated their claims, though that is not usually the case.

Immigration court records show that more asylum cases were denied over the previous five years than have been granted. In fiscal year 2016, 62 percent of asylum cases were denied, compared with 44.5 percent five years earlier. Among Mexicans and Central Americans, the approval rate is substantially lower.

ARE SOME PEOPLE JUST LOOKING FOR A BETTER LIFE?

Simply wanting a better life does not meet the international criteria to qualify for asylum. But there are people who apply anyway because it gives them some benefits, albeit temporarily, even if they ultimately lose their case.

Since the election of Mr. Trump, undocumented immigrants who have lived in the country for many years and fear deportation have been applying for asylum, knowing that they are unlikely to win, but hoping to remain in the country legally for a time.

While their application crawls through the courts, they can obtain work permits and driver's licenses.

The administration, which has taken a hard-line on immigration, has said that it is seeking to expedite asylum cases and crack down on abuse.

"There is a significant increase in terms of individuals seeking asylum," said Jennifer Higgins, an associate director at United States Immigration and Citizenship Services who handles refugee and asylum issues. "Our goal is to make sure we have a fair and efficient asylum system. Right now we have individuals exploiting it. That means legitimate applicants will suffer."

The government has also said that it will prosecute those who break immigration law.

In the case of the caravan, critics say that it would be a violation of international law to conduct speedy hearings for the caravan members at the expense of a full hearing of their claims.

"The Trump administration has made clear that asylum seekers associated with the caravan will be subjected to detention, criminal prosecutions, and rushed proceedings, in essence punishing them for seeking refugee protection," said Ms. Acer.

But Ms. Higgins said officials are assigning staff and officers to help house and process all those admitted for hearings, wherever they end up.

ALAIN DELAQUERIERE contributed research.

What It Takes to Get Asylum in the U.S.

BY MIRIAM JORDAN AND SIMON ROMERO | MAY 2, 2018

LOS ANGELES — A caravan of migrants from Central America that recently trekked to the California border has grabbed the attention of the news media and President Trump. Of the 300 or so who made it to Tijuana, at least 150 are expected to claim asylum in the United States.

"The likelihood of them getting asylum is very minimal," said Thomas Haine, a former trial attorney for Immigration and Customs Enforcement who is now in private practice in San Diego.

The biggest hurdle for the migrants is convincing an immigration judge that they belong to a particular social group — gay, transgender or a child soldier, for example — that could entitle them to asylum, since they cannot argue that they face persecution based on race, religion, nationality or political opinion.

Generally, Central American migrants are fleeing gangs, drug cartels or other violence. But fearing for one's life isn't reason enough for asylum, Mr. Haine said.

Border inspectors late Monday began allowing some asylum seekers into the country. Once processed at a port of entry, they will be transferred to a detention facility where they must pass a "credible-fear" interview.

Those who clear the first hurdle will be referred to an immigration court for hearings that can stretch for months or longer. (Those who fail can be deported.)

"In the courts is where it gets murky," said Devin T. Theriot-Orr, who teaches immigration law at Seattle University. "It's like rolling the dice."

Asylum cases filed by Latin Americans are treated differently than similar cases from Africa, Asia and the Middle East, he said. American authorities fear that granting asylum to migrants from nearby countries will encourage more to come.

Irma Rivera, 31, with her son Jesus Eduardo and daughter Soany, among other members of the migrant caravan camped out in Tijuana, Mexico, near the California border.

More than 75 percent of asylum cases that came before the immigration court from El Salvador, Honduras and Guatemala were denied between the 2012 and 2017 fiscal years, according to Syracuse University's Transactional Records Access Clearinghouse. That compares with 17 percent for Ethiopia, 20 percent for China and 25 percent for Nepal.

A sample of asylum cases, granted and denied, reflects some of the inconsistencies.

JOËL KANGUDI, 34, CONGO

Mr. Kangudi, an information technology technician and gospel singer, fled the Democratic Republic of Congo after he released a song on YouTube criticizing human rights abuses by the government. Authorities in Congo arrested Mr. Kangudi, locked him up and tortured him. He walked across a bridge to El Paso in 2017, then spent four months in a detention center in New Mexico before gaining asylum.

M. P., 30S, EL SALVADOR

M. P. and her son, J. G., fled El Salvador in 2014 after the MS-13 gang tried several times to recruit him and vowed to kill the teenager's mother unless he joined. They entered the United States illegally and applied for asylum in 2016 in Utah. A judge denied her request in March on the grounds that claims of gang violence do not qualify for asylum, but M. P. is appealing. She is unable to work and is afraid she could be deported at any moment, said her lawyer, Christina Brown of Denver. Her son is part of the same application. (They did not want be identified because they feared it could jeopardize their case.)

CRISTINA BEBAWY, 62, MOROCCO

Moroccan police officers raided the apartment where Ms. Bebawy, a teacher, participated in Bible studies in 2009. She and other women there were arrested and thrown into jail, where they were forced to undress and perform sex acts. The officers videotaped and photographed the acts, then used the footage to justify arresting the women multiple times. Ms. Bebawy received asylum after traveling to the United States on a tourist visa in 2013, according to her lawyer, Christopher Casazza, in Wayne, Pa.

CHE ERIC SAMA, 28, CAMEROON

Mr. Sama, a university student from Cameroon, applied for asylum after fleeing first to Nigeria, then traveling through Mexico to the United States border in 2015. He said he had been beaten by an anti-gay group for posting a statement in a student publication in support of gay rights in Cameroon, where same-sex sexual activity is illegal and punishable by prison. Mr. Sama, who claimed he faced the possibility of state-sanctioned harm if he was forced to return to Cameroon, had his request for asylum denied, in addition to his appeal in April. He has been deported.

YOMARA RIVAS, 27, GUATEMALA

Ms. Rivas fled to the United States with her daughter, then 4, in 2014, making a perilous trek from Guatemala to the Arizona desert. Ms.

Rivas, who was born into an impoverished family of coffee pickers, said in her asylum request that her boyfriend had become physically abusive and tried to strangle their daughter. Ms. Rivas was granted asylum before Jeff Sessions, the attorney general, signaled that he opposes giving asylum to domestic violence victims.

M. C., HONDURAS

M. C. was detained in South Texas in 2015 and requested asylum as a victim of domestic violence. She passed her credible-fear interview but then remained in detention for nine months. A judge rejected her application, contending that the Honduran government was instituting policies to address domestic violence. She filed an appeal, which was denied on similar grounds, and is appealing again. The board of immigration appeals sent the case back to the same judge, who has since retired. Her case may be heard again in 2020. M. C. cannot work and is living with her child in New Jersey, relying on family to support them. (She asked not to be identified to avoid jeopardizing her case.)

ZAHID ALI, 26, PAKISTAN

Mr. Ali was a student activist who supported autonomy for Balochistan, a region of Pakistan that some residents believe was improperly annexed in 1968. He is also a Zikri Muslim, a religious minority targeted by fundamentalists because its members do not adhere to the prophecy of Muhammad. Mr. Ali was interrogated and beaten for his political and religious beliefs. He testified during his asylum interview that returning to his homeland would be life-threatening. He was granted asylum in 2017 and was recently accepted to Columbia University.

"The asylum process is extremely difficult," Mr. Ali said, comparing it to "crossing the Bridge of Siraat," an Islamic belief that the span must be traversed to enter Paradise. "The Bridge of Siraat is as thin as the strand of hair."

MIRIAM JORDAN reported from Los Angeles, and SIMON ROMERO from Albuquerque. KIRK SEMPLE contributed reporting from Mexico City.

Is Trump's America Tougher on Asylum Than Other Western Countries?

BY PATRICK KINGSLEY | SEPT. 14, 2019

BERLIN — The Supreme Court this week allowed the Trump administration to move forward with a plan to bar most migrants, particularly Central Americans, from seeking asylum in the United States.

Under President Trump's plan, migrants cannot apply for asylum unless they have already tried — and failed — to receive it in one of the countries they passed through on their way to the United States. Guatemalans would be sent back to Mexico, for example, while people from El Salvador and Honduras would be returned to Guatemala.

Given how unsafe those countries can be for their own citizens — much less for migrants — the move has been portrayed by critics as another deviation from global rights standards under Mr. Trump. It follows his frequent attempts to expand barriers along the United States-Mexico border, as well as a deterioration in the treatment of migrants after they reach America.

But Mr. Trump's plan is also in keeping with a wider international trend of curtailing the right to asylum, as Western nations try to curb migration from the global south, where the overwhelming majority of displaced people live.

To stifle record levels of migration to Europe in 2015 and 2016, the continent's big powers reached deals with neighboring countries like Turkey to keep migrants from European shores. Australia, determined to stop maritime migration from Indonesia, now deports asylum seekers to its neighbors in the Pacific Ocean. Israel tried to send African migrants to Rwanda.

"It is currently the objective of most countries of the global north to prevent migrants" from entering their territory, said François Crépeau,

Members of a migrant caravan made up mostly of Hondurans and Cubans resting in the town plaza of Escuintla, Chiapas, Mexico, in April.

a former United Nations Special Rapporteur on migrant rights and an expert on international refugee law at McGill University.

"Probably the U.S. are taking actions a bit further from what the Europeans are doing," said Mr. Crépeau. "But the Europeans have also been very good at getting neighboring countries to do their dirty work."

DOES THE TRUMP PLAN VIOLATE INTERNATIONAL LAW?

The United Nations refugee convention of 1951 provides the basis for American asylum laws. Unlike the Trump plan, it does not prevent refugees from traveling through several countries before landing in the United States and seeking asylum.

But it does ban signatories to the convention, like the United States, from deporting asylum seekers to countries where their safety is at risk, a process formally known as "refoulement."

Most Western countries have usually interpreted this in a broad sense — refusing to deport people to countries that may not be at war, but still do not provide refugees with most of the protections required by the 1951 convention. Countries like Guatemala and Mexico, where homicide rates are high and migrants are often especially vulnerable to extortion, kidnapping and violence, could fall into that category, some experts say.

"There's a lot of evidence to suggest that the countries of the Northern Triangle and Mexico itself are not safe, and that the people passing through those countries are at risk of human rights violations," said Jeff Crisp, an expert on migration at Chatham House, a London-based research group, referring to the Central American nations of Guatemala, El Salvador and Honduras.

"Returning people to those countries could be considered in violation of the non-refoulement principle," Dr. Crisp added.

Even so, there is no international court or authority that can overrule Mr. Trump's plan. The Supreme Court's ruling is provisional, and it is expected to take up the case again. But that will take many months.

The Trump administration is also pushing Mexico and Central American countries to agree to accept migrants. Guatemala has, but the plan must still be ratified by the Guatemalan Congress.

Mexico, by contrast, has said it won't sign a so-called safe third country agreement with the United States to accept asylum claims from migrants who arrive on its soil, even if they are hoping to reach the United States.

"The court's decision is astonishing," Mexico's foreign minister, Marcelo Ebrard, said Thursday about the Supreme Court ruling.

MR. TRUMP'S PLAN HAS A CLOSE PRECEDENT, IN AUSTRALIA

Since 2012, most asylum seekers arriving in Australia by boat have been deported to processing centers in the nearby countries of Nauru and Papua New Guinea, where they are held while their asylum applications are assessed.

Rights groups like Amnesty International say that asylum seekers at these centers face severe abuse. And even if granted asylum, the migrants are still barred from resettlement in Australia. Instead, they must live in Nauru, Papua New Guinea or, in a few cases, Cambodia.

Last year, Israel was forced to cancel a comparable deal with Rwanda, in which African asylum seekers would be deported from Tel Aviv to Kigali, after a public backlash.

The concept was pioneered in 1990s by Presidents George Bush and his successor, President Clinton, who authorized American Coast Guard vessels to intercept boats loaded with Haitian refugees and take them to Guantánamo Bay for processing.

EUROPE TRIED TO DO SOMETHING SIMILAR, BUT IT DIDN'T WORK

European politicians have often spoken of sending migrants for processing in non-European countries, but the plan has never been successfully enacted.

In 2015 and 2016, more than one million migrants reached Greece from Turkey, most of them making their way to wealthier countries like Germany.

To stop this, the European Union pledged more than $6 billion to Turkey. In return, Turkey tightened up its border restrictions — and agreed to take back every migrant who subsequently landed in Greece.

Turkey did cut migration flows to Europe drastically, but only a small proportion of migrants who continued to land in Greece have been sent back. Migrants still have the opportunity to apply for asylum in Greece, or for relocation to other European countries, and many do so successfully. The Greek asylum system operates independently and is not beholden to the political agreement between the European Union and Turkey.

Meanwhile, migrants reaching Italy from Libya, another major gateway to Europe, are not returned because the country is still at war and does not recognize the 1951 convention.

One of the compounds of the Offshore Processing Center on Manus Island, Papua New Guinea.

People trying to reach Spain through its enclaves in North Africa are often forced back to Morocco without being given the chance to apply for asylum. But those who manage to cross the border into the enclaves undetected are usually allowed to lodge an asylum claim in Spain, though they are often sent back once their applications are rejected months later.

WITHIN EUROPE ITSELF, MIGRANTS MUST TECHNICALLY SEEK ASYLUM IN THE FIRST COUNTRY THEY REACH

In theory, migrants are supposed to lodge an asylum claim as soon as they reach one of the 28 member states of the European Union. Those who don't are liable to be returned to the country where they first entered the bloc — usually Greece, Italy or Spain — because European Union members theoretically trust one another to uphold the 1951 convention and treat refugees fairly.

Afghan migrants among the makeshift tents just outside Moria in the Greek Island of Lesbos.

But again, the system doesn't quite work like that in reality. Sometimes it's hard to prove that applicants passed through Greece on their way to, say, Germany. And in recent years, countries like Germany and Sweden have suspended returns to some members of the European Union, like Hungary and Greece, because of concerns about the fairness of their asylum systems.

AT EUROPE'S BEHEST, MIGRANTS ON THEIR WAY TO EUROPE ARE SOMETIMES PASSED BETWEEN AFRICAN STATES

If migrants reach Europe from Libya, they are allowed to lodge an asylum claim on European soil. But some people who haven't left Libya yet have been encouraged to fly instead to Niger, where they can apply for asylum in Europe from a country of relative safety. A similar arrangement was recently brokered with Rwanda, but has yet to formally begin.

The process is ostensibly a humanitarian one: It aims to help migrants escape war-torn Libya, where they are often prey to kidnapping, conscription, air raids, abuse and forced labor, without needing to brave the dangerous sea crossing to Italy.

But critics argue that few of them will in practice be ever resettled in Europe.

EUROPEANS ALSO BUILD FENCES AND KEEP MIGRANTS HOUSED IN POOR CONDITIONS

Like Mr. Trump, European governments have also sought to curb migration by building physical barriers along their borders. Greece has a fence lining its border with Turkey. Spain has several on its enclaves' borders with Morocco. And Hungary built one on its border with Serbia.

In addition to its deal with Turkey, the European Union and its members have often paid third parties with checkered rights records to stop migrants from reaching Europe. The bloc pays Niger to throttle migration. Spain has a deal with Morocco. And Italy enlisted Libyan militias to stifle migration across the Mediterranean.

Asylum seekers in Greece and Hungary are also mostly confined in squalid facilities. On the Greek island of Lesbos, over 10,000 people are housed in a camp built for 3,100. In Hungary, officials have repeatedly denied food for several days to dozens of asylum seekers, including children.

One notable difference between Mr. Trump and his European counterparts is the way they speak publicly about migrants. With the exception of Prime Minister Viktor Orban of Hungary and Matteo Salvini, Italy's former interior minister, European government officials have largely avoided using provocative language to stir xenophobia — while still trying to block migrants from European territory.

ELISABETH MALKIN contributed reporting from Mexico City.

CHAPTER 2

Asylum Under the Trump Administration

President Donald J. Trump was elected after a campaign built on his promise to build a wall on the U.S. border with Mexico and to clamp down on Central and South American migrants looking for refuge. And over the course of his administration, he has introduced some of the most draconian asylum laws in recent American history. The articles in this chapter explore how asylum policy has evolved and narrowed under his leadership.

Sessions Says Domestic and Gang Violence Are Not Grounds for Asylum

BY KATIE BENNER AND CAITLIN DICKERSON | JUNE 11, 2018

WASHINGTON — Attorney General Jeff Sessions on Monday made it all but impossible for asylum seekers to gain entry into the United States by citing fears of domestic abuse or gang violence, in a ruling that could have a broad effect on the flow of migrants from Central America.

Mr. Sessions's decision in a closely watched domestic violence case is the latest turn in a long-running debate over what constitutes a need for asylum. He reversed an immigration appeals court ruling that granted it to a Salvadoran woman who said she had been sexually, emotionally and physically abused by her husband.

Relatively few asylum seekers are granted permanent entry into the United States. In 2016, for every applicant who succeeded, more than 10 others also sought asylum, according to data from the Department of Homeland Security. But the process can take months or years, and tens of thousands of people live freely in the United States while their cases wend through the courts.

Mr. Sessions's decision overturns a precedent set during the Obama administration that allowed more women to claim credible fears of domestic abuse and will make it harder for such arguments to prevail in immigration courts. He said the Obama administration created "powerful incentives" for people to "come here illegally and claim a fear of return."

Asylum claims have expanded too broadly to include victims of "private violence," like domestic violence or gangs, Mr. Sessions wrote in his ruling, which narrowed the type of asylum requests allowed. The number of people who told homeland security officials that they had a credible fear of persecution jumped to 94,000 in 2016 from 5,000 in 2009, he said in a speech earlier in the day in which he signaled he would restore "sound principles of asylum and longstanding principles of immigration law."

"The prototypical refugee flees her home country because the government has persecuted her," Mr. Sessions wrote in his ruling. Because immigration courts are housed under the Justice Department, not the judicial branch of government, he has the authority to overturn their decisions.

"An alien may suffer threats and violence in a foreign country for any number of reasons relating to her social, economic, family or other personal circumstances," he added. "Yet the asylum statute does not provide redress for all misfortune."

His ruling drew immediate condemnation from immigrants' rights groups. Some viewed it as a return to a time when domestic violence was considered a private matter, not the responsibility of the government to intervene, said Karen Musalo, a defense lawyer on the case who directs the Center for Gender and Refugee Studies at the University of California Hastings College of the Law.

"What this decision does is yank us all back to the Dark Ages of human rights and women's human rights and the conceptualization of it," she said.

President Trump has long insisted that violent gang members are using the immigration system to illegally infiltrate the United States and that illegal immigrants traveled by caravan to the southern border with Mexico recently to flood into the country.

Mr. Sessions's ruling addressed those fears, but data does not support them. Since 2014, when Central Americans started surging into the United States, people seeking asylum from gang violence have only rarely succeeded. Those who were granted entry often argued their cases on multiple grounds.

The number of illegal immigrants caught at the border last year was the lowest since 1971, Border Patrol statistics showed.

Still, the White House began pressing in October for tighter asylum rules as part of any legislative package on immigration. "We effectively have a policy where if you make an unproven assertion up front of having quote unquote credible fear, that you can be released into the United States almost immediately," Stephen Miller, the White House senior policy adviser who has been the architect of Mr. Trump's immigration crackdown, said last week in an interview.

The ruling effectively closes a major avenue for asylum seekers, one dominated since 2014 by women fleeing Central America.

The Board of Immigration Appeals found in 2016 that the woman in the case — named A-B-, for her initials — was part of what the asylum system refers to as a "particular social group" because women in El Salvador are often unable to leave violent relationships and their government has not been able to protect them. She therefore qualified for asylum.

Asylum seekers can make claims that they suffered persecution related to race, religion, nationality, political opinion or their particular social group, broadly considered to include people who share a common characteristic that endangers them and whose governments will not protect them. Legal scholars have debated its definition, and some groups who have qualified include relatives of dissidents, L.G.B.T.Q. people, victims of domestic violence and people fleeing violent gangs.

Mr. Sessions narrowed that definition. "Generally, claims by aliens pertaining to domestic violence or gang violence perpetrated by nongovernmental actors will not qualify for asylum," he wrote.

Attorneys general as far back as Janet Reno, who served from 1993 to 2001, have weighed in on the use of the particular social group in asylum cases, going back and forth on how to treat issues like domestic violence.

Domestic violence victims gained eligibility after the 2014 case of a Guatemalan woman, Aminta Cifuentes. She suffered a decade of abuse by her husband, including acid burns and punches to her belly while she was eight months pregnant, forcing a premature birth. Her baby was born with bruises.

Since then, women from around the world have used the same argument to win protection in the United States. Gender-based violence was a particular problem in Central America and parts of Mexico, according to a 2015 United Nations report, which compared it to the refugee crisis emerging at the same time in Europe.

"Saying a few simple words — claiming a fear of return — is now transforming a straightforward arrest for illegal entry and immediate return into a prolonged legal process," Mr. Sessions said in his speech, to immigration judges gathered outside Washington.

Some of them said he was infringing on their ability to decide cases.

Mr. Sessions did not publicly say why he intervened in the case, which some immigration judges found troublesome, said Ashley Tabaddor, the president of the National Association of Immigration Judges.

The attorney general's ability to "exercise veto power in our decision-making is an indication of why the court needs true independence" from the Justice Department, Ms. Tabaddor said.

KATIE BENNER reported from Washington, and CAITLIN DICKERSON from New York. JULIE HIRSCHFELD DAVIS contributed reporting from Washington, and LIZ ROBBINS from New York.

Migrants Seeking Asylum Must Wait in Mexico, Trump Administration Says

BY MICHAEL TACKETT, CAITLIN DICKERSON AND AZAM AHMED | DEC. 20, 2018

WASHINGTON — The Trump administration, mired in a battle with Congress over funding of a border wall, announced on Thursday that the United States would begin requiring people seeking asylum at the southwest border to wait in Mexico for a court ruling on their cases.

After weeks of talks, the Mexican government reluctantly agreed to accept the waiting migrants, which could substantially reduce the number of people trying to gain entry into the United States and deter even those with the most credible asylum claims.

Mexican officials did not say where the immigrants would be housed or what resources they would be given, but noted that humanitarian visas and work permits would be made available.

The policy shift amounts to the boldest effort yet by the Trump administration to discourage people from seeking refuge in the United States.

Kirstjen Nielsen, the homeland security secretary, called the move "historic" and said the government was acting under emergency provisions of the Immigration and Nationality Act. The change is effective immediately.

"Today, I am announcing historic measures to bring the situation under control," Ms. Nielsen said in testimony to the House Judiciary Committee, adding that "aliens trying to game the system to get into our country illegally will no longer be able to disappear into the United States."

She said the administration was taking "lawful unilateral action to stop illegal entry now."

The policy follows a series of other limits on immigration that the administration has introduced, including separating migrant families, limiting the number of people who can apply for asylum each day, tightening requirements to win a case and restricting the locations where people can apply. (The first policy was reversed in an executive order, and the last has been temporarily blocked by a federal court.)

"It's a very significant border security development," Secretary of State Mike Pompeo said in an interview with the Fox News host Laura Ingraham.

Mr. Pompeo said the United States had "made clear to the Mexican government" the shift in policy and said Mexico would offer opportunities to "protect the rights of those migrants."

The administration has said the changes are meant to weed out people who do not qualify for asylum, but migrant rights groups argue that they would also affect those legitimately fleeing for their lives. The new policy was introduced less than a week after two Honduran teenagers were killed in an apparent robbery in Tijuana.

The boys had been staying in shelters that house asylum seekers preparing to enter the United States.

"Our concern is that this is going to endanger more lives," said Michelle Brané, the director of migrant rights and justice at the Women's Refugee Commission. "People who are waiting, and especially children, are really vulnerable."

As a result of the new curbs, shelters for asylum seekers in Mexico have been overwhelmed recently by people who would previously have been allowed into the United States on the day they presented themselves at the border, but now have to wait weeks or months.

Ms. Brané said she considered the policy "more of an abdication to our responsibility to process people seeking asylum in a fair manner."

As with many of the administration's harshest immigration plans that have been introduced with little notice — such as the travel ban and family separations — it was unclear on Thursday how exactly the new policy would apply.

The move was seen by immigration advocates as a hard-line deterrent that would force many of the migrants, even those fleeing violence and persecution, to return home. It could also give the United States a rationale to close ports of entry, the advocates said.

"I am surprised the new Mexican government would agree to carry Trump's water on this, given his harsh rhetoric toward Mexicans," said Kevin Appleby, the policy director of the Center for Migration Studies. "The administration will use this agreement moving forward to put up a virtual wall against asylum seekers. In some ways, Mexico will be paying for a wall."

The new policy will most likely alleviate pressure on American border agents who for months have argued that they are overwhelmed by the record number of migrant families seeking asylum. United States Customs and Border Protection houses the families temporarily, usually for several days, while they are processed.

Concerns about the agency's handling of children peaked this month, when a 7-year-old girl died in Border Patrol custody. The Trump administration did not take responsibility for the death, though days afterward, Kevin K. McAleenan, the commissioner of Customs and Border Protection, told Congress, "Our Border Patrol stations and ports of entry were built to handle mostly male, single adults in custody, not families or children."

A senior Department of Homeland Security official said that Thursday's announcement surprised many people in the agency's leadership, as well as the rank-and-file employees who would be charged with carrying out the policy.

Many logistical concerns had yet to be addressed, the official said, and it was still unclear whether anyone might be exempt — such as children traveling alone.

Critics of the policy predicted that it would soon be challenged in court, on the grounds that it might violate Congress's intention to allow asylum seekers into the United States. Additionally, the critics noted, the United States should adhere to international conventions that prohibit governments from returning refugees to places where they face a threat to their life or freedom.

Mr. Pompeo dismissed the chances of a legal challenge succeeding. "We are confident we are on firm ground," he said.

Mexican officials said they were told of the American decision on Thursday morning in letters from the Department of Homeland Security and the United States chargé d'affaires in Mexico, John S. Creamer. The Mexican Foreign Ministry has essentially agreed to accept the decision by the United States.

A spokesman for the ministry, Roberto Velasco, said the move did not represent an agreement between the two countries, but rather "a unilateral move by the United States that we have to respond to."

The decision to accept the asylum seekers is likely to be seen as a capitulation by the Mexican government to President Trump, who said on Twitter two weeks ago that Mexico would house asylum applicants to the United States on its soil.

Given the public enmity between Mr. Trump and Mexican leaders, the decision to turn Mexico into a waiting room for migrants seeking entry to the United States is bound to stir anger in Mexico.

Responding to a question from Representative Robert W. Goodlatte, Republican of Virginia and the House Judiciary Committee chairman, Ms. Nielsen said that the Trump administration wanted to change the policy of "catch and release" to "catch and remain" by keeping those seeking illegal entry in Mexico.

She said the policy shift was an effort "to discourage those claiming asylum fraudulently."

"We've got to fix the asylum laws," she said.

MICHAEL TACKETT reported from Washington, CAITLIN DICKERSON from New York and AZAM AHMED from Cancún, Mexico. KIRK SEMPLE contributed reporting from Mexico.

Trump Administration to Push for Tougher Asylum Rules

BY MICHAEL D. SHEAR AND ZOLAN KANNO-YOUNGS | APRIL 9, 2019

WASHINGTON — The Trump administration plans to aggressively push for tougher screening of asylum seekers that will make it vastly more difficult for migrants fleeing persecution in their home countries to win protection in the United States, a senior administration official told reporters on Tuesday.

The official said that President Trump ordered a shake-up of his top immigration officials in recent days because they were moving too slowly, or even actively obstructing, the president's desire to confront the surge of migrants at the southwestern border. The asylum changes are among many policies the president wants to put into effect with a new team in place, the official said.

Mr. Trump denied on Tuesday that one of those changes would be to restart his policy of separating migrant families at the border, though he said that the act of taking children from their parents — which drew global condemnation before he abandoned it last summer — was effective.

"Now I'll tell you something, once you don't have it, that's why you see many more people coming," Mr. Trump said. "They are coming like it's a picnic, because, 'Let's go to Disneyland.' "

The administration official, who spoke on the condition of anonymity even as Mr. Trump was making his remarks, said a modified version of family separation, in which parents are given a choice of whether to be separated or to accept indefinite detention alongside their children, continues to be under consideration.

But the so-called binary choice proposal is "not ripe for White House consideration" right now, he insisted, because the government does not currently have the detention space to hold families if the policy were put in place.

The asylum changes being envisioned could drastically alter the role that the United States plays as a refuge for people fleeing poverty, violence and war. American and international laws require it to allow migrants to request asylum once they come to the country.

But the official said that an initial assessment of the basis for a request for asylum — known as a "credible fear" screening — too often accepts the claim that the migrant was persecuted. The official also said that many more asylum seekers should be rejected during that first step.

Out of 97,728 completed interviews with migrants in the fiscal year that ended on Sept. 30, 2018, the United States Citizenship and Immigration Services confirmed a credible fear of persecution 74,677 times, according to an agency official.

Changes in the screening process could drastically lower those findings by requiring more proof from asylum seekers that they would be persecuted in their home countries. Screeners could also try to verify migrant claims by using State Department assessments of the threats that exist in those countries.

Immigrant rights advocates have feared for months that the administration would try to change the standards by which asylum seekers are judged in an effort to prevent more of them from coming into the United States.

The administration official blamed the delay in that effort on "deep state" bureaucrats at the Department of Homeland Security and even the president's own political appointees in the department, whom the official described as lacking the management skills to push Mr. Trump's agenda.

The official declined to name specific administration officials who have failed. But he made thinly veiled references to two top officials at the Department of Homeland Security: John Mitnick, the department's general counsel, and L. Francis Cissna, the head of United States Citizenship and Immigration Services.

He said there was "clearly a track record" in which the president's policies have not been advanced.

In his remarks on Tuesday, Mr. Trump falsely said that President Barack Obama had embraced the same policy of routinely separating migrant children from their parents at the border.

"President Obama had child separation," Mr. Trump said during brief remarks in the Oval Office, where he was meeting with President Abdel Fattah el-Sisi of Egypt. "I'm the one that stopped it."

Under Mr. Obama and President George W. Bush, immigration officials sometimes separated families when they had reason to question parentage or when there was evidence of child abuse. The Trump administration instituted a policy in which all families who crossed the border illegally were separated in order to allow the parents to be prosecuted under the administration's "zero tolerance" policy. More than 2,700 children were separated from their parents at the border before Mr. Trump ended the policy in June 2018.

The president's comments come after he shook up the senior ranks of the Department of Homeland Security, forcing the resignation of the secretary, Kirstjen Nielsen, and top immigration officials in a move that signaled a pending shift in immigration policies.

Also on Tuesday, the acting deputy secretary of homeland security, Claire Grady, who was next in line by law to become the acting secretary, submitted her resignation, according to a Twitter post by Ms. Nielsen. Ms. Grady's resignation paves the way for Kevin McAleenan, the commissioner of Customs and Border Protection, to take the role.

Customs and Border Protection officials this week underscored Mr. Trump's concern about illegal immigration by announcing that more than 103,000 migrants crossed the southwestern border in March without authorization, an increase from the more than 76,000 migrants who crossed in February.

"Just last month, we saw record numbers of family units and unaccompanied juvenile apprehensions in February, and unfortunately, March apprehension numbers are again record-setting and cause dire concerns for us," said Brian Hastings, the chief of law enforcement operations for the Border Patrol.

Most of the migrants — 92,000 of the 103,000 — were apprehended by Border Patrol agents, meaning they crossed in between the ports of entry.

More than 53,000 of those migrants were members of a family, Mr. Hastings said, and most of those families were from Honduras, Guatemala or El Salvador.

In the first half of fiscal year 2019, Border Patrol agents apprehended more than 385,000 migrants on the border, more than double those apprehended during the same time last year.

Mr. Hastings said the Border Patrol can generally maintain 4,500 people in its custody. But it recently counted 13,000 migrants in its facilities, and he said the overflow has led to the release of families into cities along the border.

"Backups have resulted in individuals spending additional time in Border Patrol custody in increasingly crowded conditions," Mr. Hastings said.

On Tuesday, White House officials announced that the president would appeal a judge's ruling that blocked the administration's "Migrant Protection Protocols," which require some asylum seekers to remain in Mexico while they wait for their court cases.

Mr. Trump has recently commended Mexico for doing more to stem migration to the border, but the officials said they have not seen any effect on the number of people crossing it. "The numbers aren't declining; in fact, we're still seeing 3,000 apprehensions per day," Mr. Hastings said.

Officials also revealed that among the tens of thousands of family members approaching the border each month, just 3,100 people who said they were traveling with relatives were found to have a fraudulent claim. Those people either said they had a child when the individual was over 18 or the group's members were not really related.

EILEEN SULLIVAN contributed reporting.

What Will Trump's Tough New Asylum Policy Mean for Migrants on the Border?

BY MICHAEL D. SHEAR, EILEEN SULLIVAN AND ZOLAN KANNO-YOUNGS | APRIL 17, 2019

WASHINGTON — The Trump administration now has clearance from the courts to begin a stringent new policy that will prevent many migrants outside Mexico from obtaining asylum in the United States — the latest move to stem the record-setting numbers of migrant families arriving on the southern border, many of them fleeing the threat of death in their violence-plagued home countries.

The new rule, which requires migrants to apply for and be denied asylum in at least one country on their way to the southwest border, is one of the most far-reaching immigration policies put in place so far by the Trump administration and will prevent most of those coming from outside Mexico from obtaining protections at the southwest border. Clearance from the Supreme Court this week to carry out the policy was a major victory for the Trump administration, which made restricting both legal and illegal immigration a priority.

But the new rules will not shut down the border to immigrants or lead to a sharp drop in border crossings, at least not right away. Migrants will still have options for other protections, although they will be much more difficult to obtain.

Here's a look at the state of asylum protections for migrants:

What is asylum and who can seek it?

Asylum is a legal process by which people fleeing persecution in their home country may seek to live in safety in the United States. International treaties and federal law require the government to evaluate a claim for asylum from anyone who enters the United States, whether that person arrives legally, through a port of entry or illegally by crossing the border and being apprehended.

Does the new policy mean no one from outside Mexico can apply?

Yes and no. The policy does not prohibit such applications.

It says that migrants cannot apply for asylum in the United States unless they have been denied asylum in at least one country they traveled through to get here. Mexicans are not affected. Migrants who crossed the border and applied for protections before July 16 can also continue their asylum process. That applies to thousands of migrants who came in record numbers earlier this year and were returned to Mexico under a Trump administration policy that forced migrants to wait in Mexico for the duration of their asylum case.

But Guatemalans who came after that date will first have to apply for asylum in Mexico and be denied. Hondurans and Salvadorans will have to apply and be denied in Guatemala or Mexico. Also affected are the thousands of migrants who regularly arrive from countries in Asia and Africa.

Keep in mind that the courts have not yet ruled on whether the policy is legal — that comes later. The Supreme Court merely ruled that it can remain in effect while the constitutional challenges are reviewed by the courts. That clearly will take some time.

Will migrants who are not from Mexico immediately be stopped at the border?

That's not clear. The government on Thursday issued instructions to asylum officers to begin applying the policy to any migrant who tried to cross the border on or after July 16.

But immigration lawyers who work on asylum cases said migrants will most likely still be detained in Border Patrol facilities until they are interviewed by an asylum officer at the border. If that asylum officer determines the migrant is subject to the rule, the migrant will be put into removal proceedings.

Migrants also have another option: If they can prove a fear of persecution or torture to that asylum officer, the migrants can apply for what is called a "withholding of removal." That would provide them a full immigration hearing before a judge, which could delay their deportation and provide time to apply for additional protections. But the burden of proof for that screening is much higher than the usual asylum interview.

What is the first step a migrant normally must take toward getting asylum?

People who are already in the country legally may apply for asylum directly with an agency called United States Citizenship and Immigration Services. Migrants who arrive illegally and were apprehended, or have been told they will be deported, may ask for asylum as a way of avoiding being sent home.

Soon after asking for asylum, migrants are usually interviewed by a trained asylum officer to determine whether they have a "credible fear" of persecution in their home country "on account of race, religion, nationality, membership in a particular social group or political opinion." If the officer determines that there is a "significant possibility" that the migrants will be able to prove such persecution, a court date will be set for a final determination about whether they will be granted asylum.

More than 75 percent of migrants pass the initial screening because of congressionally mandated rules that set a fairly low bar for approval to ensure that persecuted people have the opportunity to apply for refuge in the United States. Trump administration officials argue that the credible-fear screening should be far less generous.

What happens after that? Where do asylum seekers go while they wait for their case to be heard? Can they work?

Migrants who pass a credible-fear screening after being apprehended trying to cross the border illegally have often in the past been released from detention to wait for their final hearing. A huge backlog in immigration court cases — approaching 900,000 cases — has meant that some asylum seekers must wait years for their claim to be heard. After a period of time, the migrants are given permission to work legally while they wait.

The Trump administration has tried to keep more asylum seekers in detention while they wait for their day in court, in part because officials argue that many migrants disappear before their hearing, becoming permanently undocumented immigrants. The Tuesday night decision by Attorney General William P. Barr that directs immigration judges to deny some migrants a chance to post bail is part of that effort to prevent asylum seekers from getting out of jail.

Are families seeking asylum being separated?

Under federal law and court rulings, families and unaccompanied children who seek asylum may not be detained for longer than 20 days. So most are released from detention to await their asylum hearings — although the Trump administration has drafted a new regulation to hold families in detention for much longer.

Mr. Trump's decision last summer to separate migrant children from their parents at the border was an attempt to get around those restrictions. Once the children were separated and sent to shelters, the parents were subject to rules that allowed authorities to detain them for longer periods of time.

A federal judge in California halted the practice last summer and the president issued an executive order reversing the policy of routinely separating families after an uproar in which critics called it "inhumane," "cruel" and "evil." Mr. Trump has publicly said he has no plans to go back to family separations.

What do asylum seekers need to prove to be granted asylum in the United States? How many are granted asylum?

People seeking refuge in the United States must show that they have a "well-founded fear" of being persecuted if they were to return to their own country. That is often demonstrated through direct testimony about the situation they expect to face if they return home, as well as other evidence of the situation they faced before coming to the United States.

Immigration judges typically deny 80 percent of the applications, weeding out fraudulent claims and ineligible applicants. When the process was devised, there was a fairly short period between the initial screening and an appearance in immigration court. But that has changed significantly, and a backlog of hundreds of thousands of cases has led to asylum seekers waiting years to appear in court.

Do people granted asylum get public benefits?

Yes, although the Trump administration is trying to change that. Currently, if an immigration judge approves a migrant's asylum request, the migrant is eligible to receive public welfare benefits, such as food stamps and Medicaid. In some cases, the amount of benefits or the amount of time the benefits are available varies from state to state.

The Trump administration, however, has proposed a new rule that could deny public benefits to legal immigrants, including those granted asylum. Last year, the Trump administration announced that if immigrants used public assistance, such as a Section 8 housing voucher, they could be denied a green card, forcing some immigrants who are legally in the country to choose between their own welfare and the ability to live and work in the United States.

After one year, a migrant who has been granted asylum is allowed to apply for a green card to become a permanent legal resident in the United States.

What is the difference between asylum seekers and refugees?

The difference between the two types of migrants largely depends on where a person applies for safe haven. Refugees make their application outside the United States. Asylum seekers are people who are already in the country or arrive at an American port of entry. Both must prove that they realistically fear persecution in their own country.

Mr. Trump and his aides have also been trying to reduce the number of refugees who can seek protection by coming to the United States each year. In the wake of the refugee crisis created by the Syrian civil war, President Barack Obama had increased the cap on the maximum number of refugees to 110,000 before he left office. Mr. Trump has lowered the cap to 30,000.

How many people currently in the United States have asylum?

Once people are granted asylum, the government does not track when they die or move out of the country, making it difficult to know how many people currently living in the United States are in the country because they were granted asylum at some point.

According to statistics from the Department of Homeland Security, roughly 637,000 people were granted asylum between 1990 and 2017.

Most Migrants at Border With Mexico Would Be Denied Asylum Protections Under New Trump Rule

BY MICHAEL D. SHEAR AND ZOLAN KANNO-YOUNGS | JULY 15, 2019

WASHINGTON — Long before a surge of migrants from Central America overwhelmed the southwestern border, the Trump administration was already waging a broad assault on the rules determining who can seek asylum in the United States.

But on Monday, the administration announced one of its most restrictive rules yet for a system, enshrined in international law, that Mr. Trump has called "ridiculous" and "insane."

In a move that would stop virtually all Central American families who are fleeing persecution and poverty from entering the United States, Trump administration officials said they would deny asylum to migrants who failed to apply for protections in at least one country they passed through on their way north.

Under the new rule, Hondurans and Salvadorans would have to apply for — and be denied — asylum in Guatemala or Mexico before they were eligible to apply for asylum in the United States. Guatemalans would have to apply for and be denied asylum in Mexico.

The rule would effectively limit asylum protections to Mexicans and those who cross the United States' southwestern border by sea. But migrants from Honduras, El Salvador and Guatemala make up the vast majority of asylum seekers who have tried to enter the United States in record numbers this year. The Border Patrol has arrested 363,300 migrant family members from Honduras, El Salvador and Guatemala at the southwestern border so far in fiscal year 2019, compared with more than 3,200 Mexican family members.

Many Africans, Cubans and Haitians who travel through Mexico to the southwestern border would also be barred from obtaining the protections.

The administration made the announcement despite the fact that Guatemala and Mexico have refused to go along with the plan — meaning the countries have made no assurances that they will grant asylum to the migrants who are headed to the United States.

But the Trump administration, which has been negotiating fruitlessly for months with Guatemala and Mexico, gave up and made the announcement without any deal after talks with Guatemala broke down and the country's president, Jimmy Morales, backed out of a meeting on Monday at the White House. Talks with Mexico remain in flux.

The new rule is expected to be immediately challenged. Lee Gelernt, the deputy director of the American Civil Liberties Union's Immigrants' Rights Project, said in a statement that it "could not be more inconsistent with our domestic laws or international laws" and that his organization would sue swiftly.

Trump administration officials countered that the surge of migrants at the border was a growing catastrophe and that something had to be done. "This rule is a lawful exercise of authority provided by Congress to restrict eligibility for asylum," Attorney General William P. Barr said. "The United States is a generous country but is being completely overwhelmed by the burdens associated with apprehending and processing hundreds of thousands of aliens along the southern border."

For decades, the United States' willingness to serve as a place of safety for those trying to escape violence and brutality has been an expression — at times unfulfilled — of the country's values around the globe.

The asylum system, long a part of American law, was meant to give immigrants a legal opportunity to live in the United States only when they could demonstrate that they would face persecution, torture or death if they returned to their home countries.

But from the moment he came into office, Mr. Trump has called the country's asylum laws little more than permissive loopholes. "The asylum rules and laws are so bad that our Border Patrol people, who are so incredible, aren't allowed to do their jobs," the president said recently.

Mr. Trump argues that migrants are gaming the system by falsely claiming asylum and then skipping out on their court hearings. In fact, the government's own statistics show that most asylum seekers show up for their court hearings, especially if they are represented by a lawyer.

However, the waiting period to be heard in court can be years because of a backlog of more than 900,000 immigration cases. By the time immigrants show up for their hearings, they have often put down roots with children, jobs and mortgages.

Few asylum claims are granted — the Trump administration says only 20 percent are, and immigration advocates say some 40 percent are — but both sides agree that immigrants who are ultimately denied asylum often defy deportation orders and stay in the United States illegally. Previous administrations did not make it a priority to find and deport them and instead focused on illegal immigrants who had committed serious crimes.

But Mr. Trump and his immigration brain trust — led by Stephen Miller, the chief architect of his border policies — say such a loose policy lures people to the United States. They are determined to break it by any means necessary.

"Folks are incentivized by the gaps in our legal framework to come to the United States right now," Kevin McAleenan, the acting homeland security secretary, said recently in an interview. "That's a group we don't think should be coming, don't think should be crossing unlawfully, don't think should be in the hands of smugglers and enriching criminal organizations."

"That is a flow we think should stop," he said.

Although Monday's announcement was Mr. Trump's most wide-ranging effort to date, the administration has worked to keep migrants from seeking asylum in dozens of actions by multiple agencies.

At the United States Citizenship and Immigration Services, employees who do the initial screening interviews for asylum seekers have been issued new guidance and training manuals to make it harder for applicants to pass the screening.

At the State Department, officials have created detailed maps showing the levels of crime in Central American countries so that the screeners can challenge asylum seekers who claim to be fleeing from danger.

At the Justice Department, Mr. Barr has issued new rules to deny bail to people in jail for immigration violations who then claim asylum. Jeff Sessions, Mr. Barr's predecessor, ruled that fleeing from domestic violence and gangs would no longer qualify someone for asylum, though the rule has been blocked by the courts.

At the ports of entry, Border Patrol agents have so significantly slowed the processing of asylum applicants that many migrants who have made the journey to the United States border simply give up.

The administration has yet to succeed in one of its biggest anti-asylum targets: overturning a two-decade-old court-ordered consent decree that limits the detention of migrant children to no more than 20 days and requires the children to be treated humanely. Mr. Miller, in particular, has been pushing for legislation or new regulations that would allow the government to detain children for longer than the 20 days.

The administration has also been stymied in a previous effort to declare that any migrant who crosses the southern border between the official ports of entry as ineligible for asylum. That rule was blocked by the courts.

But the courts have allowed the Department of Homeland Security to begin ordering asylum seekers to wait in Mexico for their cases to proceed, many with little access to lawyers. More than 13,000 migrants looking for asylum protections are now waiting just across the border in Mexico, according to the most recent Department of Homeland Security statistics.

So far, the administration's efforts have largely failed to stem the flow of migrants. In May, more than 144,000 surged across the border, a majority of whom were from Honduras, Guatemala and El Salvador. While arrests declined in June by 28 percent, officials estimate that by the end of the year, nearly a million migrants may have crossed the southwestern border, most of them hoping to stay permanently by claiming asylum.

Under the new rule, migrants would still be allowed to apply for asylum at the southwestern border if they have proof that they applied and were denied the protections in at least one country they traveled through. Filippo Grandi, the United Nations high commissioner for refugees, released a statement on Monday that he was "deeply concerned" by the new rule. "It will put vulnerable families at risk," Mr. Grandi said. "It will undermine efforts by countries across the region to devise the coherent, collective responses that are needed."

Representative Bennie Thompson, Democrat of Mississippi and the chairman of the House Homeland Security Committee, described the regulation as "xenophobic and racist."

"Plain and simple, this is the president lashing out in an attempt to keep those seeking safety out of the country," Mr. Thompson said in a statement.

At a news conference in Mexico City, Marcelo Ebrard, the foreign minister, did not say what Mexico would do with asylum seekers who were denied the right to petition for protections in the United States. But he did have subtle criticism for the new rule.

"Mexico doesn't agree with measures that limit access to asylum and refuge for those people who fear for their life or security in their countries of origin because of persecution," Mr. Ebrard said.

ELISABETH MALKIN and **KIRK SEMPLE** contributed reporting from Mexico City.

The U.S. and Guatemala Reached an Asylum Deal: Here's What It Means

BY KIRK SEMPLE | JULY 28, 2019

MEXICO CITY — President Trump has made migration the defining issue in the relationship between his administration and the governments of Central America and Mexico.

He has pressed the region's leaders to reduce the number of migrants heading north and crossing the southwest border of the United States, even going so far as to freeze hundreds of millions of dollars in development aid to Central America.

One of his goals has been to get those countries to absorb more asylum seekers. On Friday, Mr. Trump made a surprise announcement that the United States had signed an agreement with Guatemala that would require asylum seekers who travel through that country to first seek refuge there.

The deal represents a major shift from longstanding American policy and would be extraordinarily rare by international standards. Many details have not been disclosed, and critics in both the United States and Guatemala have threatened to go to court to try to derail it.

But if successfully put in place, the agreement could have profound effects on migrant flows in the hemisphere.

This is what we know about it.

HOW WOULD THE AGREEMENT FUNCTION?

Every month, tens of thousands of migrants — from Latin America and around the world — have been making their way north through Central America in the hopes of crossing into the United States. An increasing number have sought sanctuary in the United States, overwhelming the American asylum system and infuriating Mr. Trump, who has tried to limit their ability to win American protection.

Migrants from Guatemala walking along the Mexican side of the border wall, looking for an opportunity to enter the United States to seek asylum.

The American government's latest tactic is the agreement with Guatemala.

Known as a "safe third country agreement," the deal would make asylum seekers ineligible for protection in the United States if they had traveled through Guatemala and did not first apply for asylum there. Under the agreement, the American authorities would be allowed to return those migrants to Guatemala, relieving pressure on the American immigration system.

The arrangement would largely prevent people from Honduras and El Salvador, two of the main sources of migrants at the moment, from seeking American asylum. It would also block large numbers of asylum seekers from elsewhere in Latin America and around the world who travel by land to the United States via Guatemala. Guatemalan and Mexican asylum seekers, however, would not be affected.

Safe third country agreements are rare. The United States signed such a deal with Canada in 2002. The European Union has one with Turkey that allows asylum seekers who arrive at the Greek border to be returned to Turkey.

But it appears that no such agreement has been signed with a nation that is as ill-equipped as Guatemala to deal with asylum seekers and keep them safe, experts say. Though homicide rates there have fallen sharply in the last decade, the country remains among the deadliest in the world. Crime, impunity and corruption are rife, and critics argue that it is unable to meet the safety requirements demanded by the deal.

The State Department has issued alerts about the rampant violence and frail law-enforcement system in the country.

"Violent crime, such as armed robbery and murder, is common," the State Department warns in its current travel advisory for Guatemala. "Gang activity, such as extortion, violent street crime, and narcotics trafficking, is widespread. Local police may lack the resources to respond effectively to serious criminal incidents."

IS EVERYONE ON BOARD?

Trump administration officials have said that the agreement will go into effect in the next several weeks. But there are several significant obstacles in its way.

Critics in both the United States and Guatemala will almost certainly file legal challenges that could delay, alter or eviscerate the deal.

Opposition to the agreement is widespread in Guatemala, where the Constitutional Court ruled recently that the Guatemalan government needed congressional approval to make a safe third country deal with the United States. That ruling, which came amid negotiations between the Trump administration and the administration of the Guatemalan president, Jimmy Morales, prompted Mr. Trump to threaten the Central American nation with punitive tariffs, a travel ban and

Merchants crossing the Guatemala–Mexico border.

taxes on the remittances sent home by Guatemalan migrants in the United States.

On Friday, Mr. Morales seemed to be trying to skirt the court ruling by avoiding the use of the term "safe third country" in his statement on the deal. But the Trump administration did use the term, giving impetus to potential legal challenges in Guatemala.

There are also several steps the United States government must take before the agreement can be put into effect.

The Justice Department and the Department of Homeland Security would have to certify that Guatemala has a "full and fair" asylum system, and is able to protect asylum seekers from other countries if the United States sends them there.

The logistics of the plan are also still being determined. What would be the process for determining that a migrant should be returned to Guatemala? How many migrants could be sent back each week? How would they be transported?

A draft of the plan circulating among American officials suggests that initially, a limited number of migrants would be sent to Guatemala each week — perhaps several hundred in a month. That would be a tiny fraction of the tens of thousands that have been seeking asylum each month at the border with Mexico.

A delay in putting the agreement into effect, or a limiting of its scope, would almost certainly disappoint Mr. Trump. Still, administration officials hope that any migrant returns, no matter how small in number, would serve as a deterrent to others contemplating making the trip to the United States.

WOULD THE DEAL WORK?

To answer this question, let's look at some numbers.

Last year, about 62,000 people from El Salvador and Honduras petitioned for asylum in the United States, according to the United Nations. Most of them entered the country through the southwest border.

By comparison, a total of 257 people sought asylum in Guatemala.

The Migration Policy Institute in Washington called the Guatemalan asylum system "embryonic."

Should the deal stand, the possible surge in applications would force Guatemala to set up a robust asylum processing system in a very short period of time.

Beyond the particulars of Guatemala's case, safe third country agreements have had mixed success and "have generally proven difficult to enforce for a mix of practical and legal reasons," the Migration Policy Institute said in a commentary. Such challenges have included proving that the asylum seeker transited the safe country in the first place.

In the three years following the 2016 signing of the agreement between the European Union and Turkey, about 2,400 people were returned from Greece to Turkey out of about 145,600 arrivals in Greece, the institute said.

But an even bigger question about the new United States-Guatemala agreement is whether the Guatemalan authorities could honor the promise of keeping asylum seekers safe. And few are betting on that.

MICHAEL SHEAR contributed reporting from Washington.

'This Takes Away All Hope': Rule Bars Most Applicants for Asylum in U.S.

BY AZAM AHMED AND PAULINA VILLEGAS | SEPT. 12, 2019

MEXICO CITY — Thousands of people fleeing persecution, most from Central America, line up at the United States' southern border every day hoping for asylum. They wait for months, their names slowly crawling up a hand-drawn list until they are allowed to present their case to American immigration authorities.

After the United States Supreme Court issued an order this week, almost none of them will be eligible for asylum.

The Supreme Court on Wednesday allowed the Trump administration to enforce new rules that bar asylum applications from anyone who has not already been denied asylum in one of the countries they traveled through on their way to the United States.

The rule is among the most stringent measures taken by this administration in its battle to halt migration, upending decades of asylum and humanitarian norms. It is likely to affect hundreds of thousands of migrants traveling through Mexico to reach the United States: Eritreans and Cameroonians fleeing political violence. Nicaraguans and Venezuelans fleeing repression.

And the largest group of all: Hondurans, Salvadorans and Guatemalans escaping the twin scourges of poverty and gangs.

"This takes away all hope," said Eddie Leonardo Caliz, 34, who left San Pedro Sula in Honduras with his wife and two kids three months ago to try to escape gang violence, and spoke from a shelter in southern Mexico. With measures like this, he said, the Trump administration "is depriving us of the opportunity to be safe."

The new rule, which has been allowed to take effect pending legal challenges, is consistent with the Trump administration's posture of hostility and rejection for those seeking protection in the United States.

Whether by separating families of migrants, by drastically limiting the number of asylum applications accepted on a given day or by returning those entering the United States to Mexico to await their hearings, the administration has shown a dogged determination to discourage migration.

And it has put tremendous pressure on Mexico to help meet its goal, threatening months ago to escalate tariffs on all Mexican goods if the nation did not buffer the surge of migrants heading to the United States from Central America and elsewhere.

Mexico responded. This week, when Mexican and American officials met in Washington to discuss progress on the issue, the Mexican delegation took great pains to show how its crackdown along its border with Guatemala and throughout the country has reduced migration flows to the United States by more than 50 percent in the last three months.

Mexico's actions, though applauded by Trump administration officials this week, have overwhelmed its troubled migration system. The number of individuals applying for asylum in Mexico has already skyrocketed in the last few years, as the United States has tightened its borders.

This rule could add to that burden, with many more applying for asylum in Mexico, despite the danger of remaining in Mexico. Violence there has soared to the highest levels in more than two decades. Stories of migrants kidnapped along the border abound, as criminal organizations await their return from the United States or pick them off as they attempt to cross the border.

Several migrants who are making their way north said in interviews on Thursday that the new rule would not deter them. For most, the hope of a new life in the United States outweighed whatever legal worries might lie ahead.

"I know things are getting more and more complicated in the U.S.," said Noel Hernández, 21, who was staying at a migrant shelter in Guatemala after leaving his home in Tegucigalpa, in Honduras, a few days ago.

"It's like flipping a coin," he said. "I either win or I lose."

Others said they would try to make it in Mexico, despite the violence, or in Guatemala, a nation with a barely functional asylum system.

Central American migrants at the Amar shelter in Nuevo Laredo in July.

Oscar Daniel Rodríguez, 33, from San Salvador, has been in Guatemala with his wife and 3-year-old son for a month now, and says he will apply for asylum there.

He had applied for asylum in Mexico during a previous trek, and was rejected. If he is denied in Guatemala, he will try again in Mexico, he said. If they deny him again, he will try the United States.

"No matter how long it takes, and how long we have to wait, what we want is to give our son a better future," he said.

Mexican asylum applicants, who don't have to transit through another country to reach the United States, are not impacted by the new policy.

Like past efforts by the Trump administration to curb migration, Wednesday's order could prove a burden for Mexico.

A senior Mexican official who spoke anonymously because the government has not addressed the issue publicly said that, for now, individuals who seek to apply will not fall under a previous provision, called

Migrant Protection Protocol. That provision sends those applying for asylum in the United States back to Mexico to await their hearings.

Instead, migrants will either have to apply for another form of relief in the United States — with a higher bar for acceptance and fewer protections — or be deported back to their home countries.

Mexico is already playing host to tens of thousands of migrants awaiting their asylum hearings in the United States. Its migrant detention facilities can be overcrowded, unsafe and unsanitary.

Asylum applications there have soared in the last year, reaching about 50,000 through August, compared to fewer than 30,000 applications in the same period a year ago. This has placed a strain on Mexican society and on a system ill-equipped to handle such demand.

"We see detention centers crammed with migrants and children, riots, social problems arising, human rights abuses, and rising xenophobia among Mexicans," said Jorge Chabat, a professor of international relations the University of Guadalajara. "The Mexican government has then little to no other choice but to design long-term migration policies to deal with the large number of migrants coming and staying now in Mexico."

"There is not much else we can do," he added, ruefully, "besides maybe lighting a candle for the Virgin of Guadalupe and praying for Trump not to be re-elected."

The initial rule to block asylum sent shock waves among immigrant rights advocates when it was issued by the Trump administration in July of this year. It was almost immediately challenged in lawsuits.

The initiative was a unilateral move by the Trump administration after failed negotiations with Mexico and Guatemala to reach deals, called safe third country agreements, that would have required those countries to absorb asylum seekers who passed through them on their way to the United States.

Though Guatemala eventually caved to the administration's pressure, and reached a safe third country agreement with the United States, Mexico remained firm in its refusal.

Now, with the Supreme Court allowing the asylum rule to go into effect, some feel the United States got what it wanted anyway — without the other countries' consent.

"This is the latest step in terms of Trump's policies to push Mexico to become a safe third country, and to make a big chunk of the migration flow stay in Mexico permanently and deter them from traveling north," said Raúl Benítez, a professor of international relations at the National Autonomous University of Mexico.

The Mexican government, for its part, insists the move is not the same as a safe third country arrangement, which would require a bilateral agreement and would automatically send the majority of asylum seekers back to Mexico for good.

Neither Mexican officials nor independent experts believe it will lead to an immediate influx of returnees to Mexico. Instead, it could leave those who have been returned to Mexico while they await hearings more likely to stay because they will not be granted protection in the United States.

While the new rules will inhibit most migrants from applying for asylum, there are other forms of protected status that remain open to them, though the bar to entry is much higher.

Under current asylum law, individuals must show a credible fear, which is figured to be a 10 percent chance that they will face persecution if sent back home. The threshold for the two remaining protections now — so-called withholding status and qualification under the convention against torture — is reasonable fear. To qualify, the applicant must show a probability of being persecuted back home that is greater than 50 percent.

"The people affected by this policy are the most vulnerable — those without lawyers and those without knowledge of the system," said Aaron Reichlin-Melnick, an immigration attorney with the Immigration Council. "Those without lawyers are being asked to meet a standard almost impossible for someone uneducated in asylum law to meet."

DANIELE VOLPE contributed reporting from Guatemala City.

U.S. Agreement With El Salvador Seeks to Divert Asylum Seekers

BY ZOLAN KANNO-YOUNGS AND ELISABETH MALKIN | SEPT. 20, 2019

WASHINGTON — The Trump administration signed an agreement with the government of El Salvador on Friday that could force Central American migrants traveling through El Salvador to seek refuge in that violent and dangerous country instead of in the United States.

The agreement is a win for President Trump and his hard-line immigration policies, and it gives him another ally in Central America as he tries to block migrants from seeking asylum at the southwestern border. Washington has signed a similar agreement with Guatemala.

But details on the agreement with El Salvador remain vague, including what steps need to be taken to carry it out.

After signing the accord with Alexandra Hill, El Salvador's foreign minister, the acting secretary of homeland security, Kevin K. McAleenan, promoted the deal as a broader collaboration that included United States investment into El Salvador's asylum system. He provided few details.

"Individuals crossing through El Salvador should be able to seek protections there, and we want to enforce the integrity of that process throughout the region but with the broader part of our partnership for addressing migration flows," Mr. McAleenan said.

Mr. McAleenan has prioritized such agreements to slow the flow of migrants fleeing corruption and persecution in their home countries by forcing them to seek protection elsewhere. Fewer migrants cross through El Salvador, however, compared with Guatemala.

Even without the buy-in of other nations, the Trump administration has taken perhaps the most significant step to curb asylum seeking at the United States border by forbidding applications from would-be asylum seekers who have traveled through another country on their way to America. Under that action, only those already denied asylum in a third country can appeal for it from the United States.

The Supreme Court allowed the administration to enforce policy, but it is still being challenged.

And while Mr. McAleenan and Mr. Trump have discussed the accords with Central American countries as crucial factors in the reduction of apprehensions at the border, they have yet to actually be put in place.

When the United States signed its "safe-third country" agreement with Guatemala, Trump administration officials said migrants would start being returned to that country in August under the agreement. Officials from both countries have walked that label back because it carries a stigma, calling the label a "cooperative agreement" instead.

Guatemala's Constitutional Court ruled that lawmakers in the capital, Guatemala City, needed to approve the policy before it could be carried out, and that has yet to happen. The administration has also failed to get Mexico to sign such an agreement.

Human rights advocates say it makes no sense to ask migrants to seek protection in countries like El Salvador and Guatemala, which are among the most dangerous, gang-ridden places in the world.

Tens of thousands of Salvadorans have been displaced from their homes, and the number of disappearances suggests that the official homicide rate may be considerably higher than the numbers reported by the police.

In 2018, about 46,800 Salvadorans sought asylum worldwide, ranking the country sixth in the world for new asylum seekers. In addition, according to a government study supported by the United Nations high commissioner for refugees, at least 71,500 Salvadorans have been internally displaced by violence. Overall, about 150,000 Salvadorans have become refugees or sought asylum in recent years.

"All these rules, agreements and procedural hurdles are creating a paper wall on the southern border, one that is just as inhumane, immoral, and illegal as one made of metal or bricks," said Eric

Schwartz, the president of Refugees International, an advocacy organization. "When history looks back on this period in the United States, the judgment will be harsh and unsparing."

Since taking office in June, President Nayib Bukele of El Salvador has moved quickly to try to bring down the country's homicide rate, sending the military into its most violent areas.

Although it had already begun to fall since 2017, when it was the highest in the world, according to the United Nations office on drugs and crime, the first three months of Mr. Bukele's presidency showed a continued drop. According to Roberto Valencia, a Salvadoran reporter who analyzes homicide statistics released by the National Civil Police, the homicide rate in August was the lowest since 2013.

In 2017, there were 10.8 homicides a day in El Salvador, which has a population of about 6.5 million. In July, there were five homicides each day, and 4.2 in August, according to Mr. Valencia.

Still, Ms. Hill acknowledged the dire conditions.

"This is El Salvador's responsibility because El Salvador has not been able to give our people enough security or opportunities so that they can stay and thrive in El Salvador," Ms. Hill said.

She also emphasized that the Bukele administration sought to prevent Salvadorans from making the dangerous trip to the United States, referring to a photograph of a father and daughter from El Salvador who drowned in June in the Rio Grande.

"That hit El Salvador in the heart," Ms. Hill said. "And it hit the United States in the heart. And that's what we're trying to avoid."

Mr. McAleenan committed to helping El Salvador build its system with the United Nations high commissioner for refugees.

The commissioner was not consulted on this latest agreement, and Giovanni Bassu, the regional representative for Central America and Cuba, said he had not seen the agreement.

He also said El Salvador's "very small" asylum office does not have any dedicated staff. Only 30 people applied for asylum in the country last year; 18 of those applications are still pending.

"My main message is that they have other priorities that the state should be investing in," Mr. Bassu said. "I think rightfully the Salvadoran government is investing its resources where there is a need," including managing internal displacement and addressing the root causes of migration.

It also remains unclear what El Salvador will receive from the United States. For the agreement with Guatemala, the United States agreed to invest $40 million in aid to help build the country's asylum system. Ms. Hill said the El Salvador government would need help combating gangs, as well as more economic opportunities.

Mr. Bukele has previously lobbied the United States to provide the 200,000 Salvadorans living in the United States with temporary protected status for 20 years. The Trump administration's attempts to remove those protections have been blocked in court, but that status will expire in January.

On Friday, Ms. Hill again said those Salvadorans needed help, but neither she nor Mr. McAleenan said it was part of the agreement.

"The T.P.S. is temporary," she said. "But there are also other measures that we are working on to find a permanent solution to this issue."

ZOLAN KANNO-YOUNGS reported from Washington, and ELISABETH MALKIN from Mexico City. MICHAEL D. SHEAR contributed reporting Washington.

New Trump Administration Proposal Would Charge Asylum Seekers an Application Fee

BY ZOLAN KANNO-YOUNGS AND MIRIAM JORDAN | NOV. 8, 2019

WASHINGTON — The Trump administration on Friday proposed hiking a range of fees assessed on those pursuing legal immigration and citizenship, as well as for the first time charging those fleeing persecution for seeking protection in the United States.

The rule, which will be published on Thursday and will have a monthlong comment period, would increase citizenship fees more than 60 percent, to $1,170 from $725, for most applicants. For some, the increase would reach 83 percent. The government would also begin charging asylum seekers $50 for applications and $490 for work permits, a move that would make the United States one of four countries to charge people for asylum.

It would also increase renewal fees for hundreds of thousands of participants of the Deferred Action for Childhood Arrivals program, also known as DACA. That group, known as "Dreamers," would need to pay $765, rather than $495, for a renewal request. The fee hike comes days before the Supreme Court is scheduled to hear arguments on the validity of President Trump's justification to terminate DACA.

"Once again, this administration is attempting to use every tool at its disposal to restrict legal immigration and even U.S. citizenship," said Doug Rand, a founder of Boundless Immigration, a technology company in Seattle that helps immigrants obtain green cards and citizenship. "It's an unprecedented weaponization of government fees."

Kenneth T. Cuccinelli II, the acting director of United States Citizenship and Immigration Services, said in a statement that the proposed changes would alleviate an "overextended system," allowing his agency to address an annual deficit of nearly $1.3 billion a year.

Former agency officials and immigration lawyers, however, said the decision to charge asylum seekers erased a long-held principle of not placing a financial burden on some of the world's most vulnerable people seeking protection.

"There was a recognition that the likelihood of their ability to pay is really in question," said Barbara Strack, a former chief of the agency's refugee affairs division under Presidents George W. Bush and Barack Obama. "The only way to understand this is as a part of the administration's campaign of hostility against the asylum program."

The Trump administration has already tried to limit immigration to the United States through numerous policies that favor those with more wealth. This summer, Mr. Cuccinelli announced a "public charge" rule that would deny poor immigrants green cards if they were deemed likely to use government benefit programs like food stamps and subsidized housing. Last month, the administration said it would deny visas to immigrants who cannot prove they will have health insurance or the ability to pay for medical costs once they become permanent residents of the United States.

Federal judges have blocked both policies from taking effect as legal challenges play out.

The White House has also specifically targeted asylum seekers arriving at the southwestern border. More than 50,000 have been forced to wait in Mexico while their immigration cases are adjudicated, and the administration is trying to deny protections to migrants who fail to apply for asylum in at least one country on their way to the border.

Mr. Cuccinelli has often said that the agency is strapped for resources as it works to tackle a backlog of more than one million cases in immigration court.

United States Citizenship and Immigration Services, he said in a statement, "is required to examine incoming and outgoing expenditures, just like a business, and make adjustments based on that analysis." He said the proposed changes would help an "overextended system."

According to the proposal, the additional revenue would help replenish the agency's budget after Mr. Trump transferred more than $207 million of its funding to Immigration and Customs Enforcement, the agency responsible for deportations and the long-term detention of migrants.

Officials with the Department of Homeland Security said in the proposal that the transfer would support investigating "immigration fraud." ICE agents were deployed to the southwestern border this year to conduct DNA tests on migrants to weed out what administration officials described as "fraudulent families" — children traveling with adults who are not their parents.

Along with the various fee increases, the proposal would also eliminate fee waivers that Citizenship and Immigration Services currently grants to those experiencing certain financial hardships.

If any of the new fees or fee increases go into effect, they will almost certainly prompt legal challenges.

Immigration advocates balked at the notion that the proposal was meant to cover the agency's deficit, with some speculating that the changes were politically motivated to reduce the number of immigrants who are able to become naturalized citizens before the 2020 presidential election.

"This administration is working assiduously to put up more barriers to immigrants," said Melissa Rodgers, the director of programs at the Immigrant Legal Resource Center in San Francisco.

She described the naturalization fee increases as part of "a pattern of attack" by the Trump administration "to undermine the opportunity for immigrants to become citizens."

"It's saying if you aren't wealthy, you are not welcome here," she added.

ZOLAN KANNO-YOUNGS is the homeland security correspondent, based in Washington. He covers immigration, border issues, cyber security, transnational crime and other national security threats.

MIRIAM JORDAN is a national immigration correspondent. She reports from a grassroots perspective on the impact of immigration policy. She has been a reporter in Mexico, Israel, Hong Kong, India and Brazil.

CHAPTER 3

Life on the Border

The asylum process is long and complicated, sometimes keeping individuals and families tied up in judicial hearings for years before a decision is reached. The articles in this chapter explore the lives of individuals waiting for asylum, those stranded at the border of the United States and Mexico, as well as those who have been admitted into America and exist in a state of limbo as they await the results that will determine their fate.

Gays Seeking Asylum in U.S. Encounter a New Hurdle

BY DAN BILEFSKY | JAN. 28, 2011

ROMULO CASTRO considered attending his asylum interview in Rosedale, Queens, dressed as Fidela Castro, a towering drag queen in six-inch stilettos, a bright green poodle skirt and a mane of strawberry blond hair. In the end, Mr. Castro, 34, opted for what he described as understatement: pink eye shadow, a bright pink V-neck shirt and intermittent outbursts of tears.

After years of trying to conceal his sexual orientation back home in Brazil (where Fidela never made an appearance), Mr. Castro had been advised by his immigration lawyer that flaunting it was now his best weapon against deportation.

"I was persecuted for being fruity, a boy-girl, a fatso, a faggot — I felt like a monster," said Mr. Castro, who reported being raped by an uncle at age 12, sexually abused by two police officers, and hounded and beaten by his peers before fleeing to the United States in 2000. "Here, being gay was my salvation. So I knew I had to put on the performance of my life."

Amid international outcry over news of the Czech Republic's testing the veracity of claims of purportedly gay asylum seekers by attaching genital cuffs to monitor their arousal while they watched pornography, some gay refugees and their advocates in New York are complaining that they can be penalized for not outwardly expressing their sexuality. While asylum-seekers and rights groups here expressed relief that use of the so-called erotic lie detector is impossible to imagine in the United States, some lamented in recent interviews that here too, homosexuals seeking asylum may risk being dismissed as not being gay enough.

The very notion of "gay enough," of course, or proving one's sexuality through appearance, dress and demeanor, can be offensive — and increasingly androgynous fashions and the social trend known as metrosexuality have blurred identities in many people's minds.

"Judges and immigration officials are adding a new hurdle in gay asylum cases that an applicant's homosexuality must be socially visible," said Lori Adams, a lawyer at Human Rights First, a nonprofit group, who advises people seeking asylum based on sexuality. "The rationale is that if you don't look obviously gay, you can go home and hide your sexuality and don't need to be worried about being persecuted."

Jhuan Marrero, 18, who was born in Venezuela but has lived — illegally — in New York since he was 4, said the immigration officer at his asylum interview last week challenged him about his macho demeanor.

"I was brought up by my parents to walk and talk like a man," said Mr. Marrero, who volunteers at the Queens Pride House, a gay and lesbian center in Jackson Heights.

"The officer said: 'You're not a transsexual. You don't look gay. How are you at risk?' I insisted that if I was sent back to Venezuela, I would speak out about being gay and suffer the consequences."

Victoria Neilson, legal director of the New York-based Immigration Equality, which provides assistance to asylum seekers, recalled the case of a 21-year-old lesbian who had been threatened with gang rape in her native Albania to cure her of her sexual orientation, but was initially denied asylum, Ms. Neilson said, because she was young, attractive and single, apparently not conforming to the officer's stereotype of a lesbian. (A judge later granted her asylum, Ms. Neilson said.)

Chris Rhatigan, a spokeswoman for the United States Citizenship and Immigration Services, said each case is examined individually, both for evidence of sexual orientation and the conditions of the country of origin. While she declined to comment specifically on the examples cited by Mr. Marrero and Ms. Neilson, Ms. Rhatigan said such behavior by immigration officers would not be condoned.

"We don't say that someone is insufficiently gay or homosexual, whatever that would mean, or that he or she could be saved by hiding his or her homosexuality," Ms. Rhatigan said. "Sexual preference is an immutable characteristic. It is something an individual can't or shouldn't change."

Citizenship and Immigration Services received 38,000 asylum applications between October 2009 and September 2010, but the agency does not track how many cite being gay or lesbian as a reason. People may qualify for asylum if they can demonstrate past persecution or a well-founded fear of future persecution based on membership in a particular social group; in 1994, the scope of the law was expanded to specifically include homosexuals.

Illegal immigrants seeking asylum are interviewed by immigration officers, who can either approve their applications or refer them to an immigration judge. Gay applicants must marshal evidence of their sexual orientation and their risk of persecution, like affidavits from same-sex partners or police and medical reports of abuse. But legal experts said that the burden of proof can be difficult for people from places like Saudi Arabia or Iran where homosexuality is punishable by death and it can be dangerous to be openly gay or report an anti-gay hate crime — or from Western countries that are believed to be sexually tolerant.

Advocates said the situation had gotten worse amid the troubled economy and high unemployment rates, citing anti-immigrant sentiments and a desperation that had led some straight immigrants to feign being gay in hopes of winning asylum.

One lawyer recalled a recent client who applied for asylum on the basis of sexual orientation, then showed up a few weeks later with his wife, seeking help with a green card. In 2009, Steven and Helena Mahoney of Kent, Wash., pleaded guilty to charges stemming from a consulting business in which, among other things, they coached straight people on how to file gay asylum claims.

For fees of up to $4,000, the Mahoneys provided asylum seekers with dramatic (if fictional) stories of anti-gay persecution, along with lists of gay bars and maps of the gay pride parade route in Seattle to help them pass as gay, according to federal prosecutors. Mr. Mahoney was sentenced to 18 months in prison, Mrs. Mahoney, to 6 months.

Ms. Rhatigan, the immigration spokeswoman, said that judges and immigration officers were highly trained to assess the evidence in asylum cases, and that each case was carefully scrutinized for signs of fraud.

Even in cases where the persecution is real, experts said, coming from a country perceived as sexually liberal can be a disadvantage.

Mr. Castro, the son of an army officer in a staunchly conservative Roman Catholic family, said he was initially advised by immigration lawyers in Washington and New York not to bother applying for asylum since he came from Brazil, a country that has developed a reputation for gay pride parades, Carnival pageantry and drag queens.

In 1999, Mr. Castro was accosted by two police officers after leaving a gay club in the northeastern city of São Luís, Maranhão, according to his asylum application. He said they forced him to perform oral sex. When he started to sob, he said, one of the officers dangled a bag of cocaine and threatened to frame him.

Depressed and despondent, Mr. Castro said he considered the priesthood, and prayed every day; he also tried to date women. After a year, he decided to flee to the United States. He obtained a tourist visa, which he overstayed by eight years.

Last year, Mr. Castro, now a massage therapist living in Jackson Heights, decided to apply for asylum so that he would not have to live in fear of being deported.

The day of his interview in 2009, he was shaking. "I thought, 'They will never let me stay,' " he said. "I cried."

He said the officer was initially unsmiling and intimidating. "I figured I was doomed," he said.

He showed her the affidavit his older brother had written begging the United States to keep Romulo "forever away from us" to prevent him from shaming the family. He shared a letter from his psychiatrist confirming that he took antidepressants for the post-traumatic stress disorder caused by his abuse. He came armed with a thick stack of articles detailing episodes of persecution of gays in Brazil.

Coached by his lawyer to be anything but bashful, he also produced several photographs at the end of the interview of his alter ego, Fidela, decked out in a tiny, strapless, black-satin cocktail dress dangling a stiletto heel from atop a giant pink float.

In June 2009, he was awarded asylum. He got a green card last summer.

Fleeing Violence in Honduras, a Teenage Boy Seeks Asylum in Brooklyn

BY JOHN LELAND | DEC. 5, 2014

HERE IS ALEJANDRO RODRIGUEZ, 15, on a Sunday afternoon in Sunset Park, walking under a tree with his father, wishing he were playing soccer with his friends. And here he is on a rainy afternoon at Franklin Delano Roosevelt High School in Brooklyn, spiky bangs pushed down toward his dark brown eyes, raising his hand in a class for English-language learners.

"I eat pizza *sometimes*," Alejandro said, filling in the last word.

He speaks guardedly around grown-ups, and stares into his smartphone when he gets bored or uncomfortable. He likes math, soccer and the band Linkin Park.

In one month this spring, gangs in his hometown in Honduras tortured and killed seven or eight children his age or younger, then threatened to kill him and his brother if they did not join the gang. The boys had no adults to protect them.

Now Alejandro, whose given name is Isaid, is in a deportation proceeding, one round face in the surge of unaccompanied minors who poured across the border from Central America this spring and summer.

Immigration agents picked up 68,541 unaccompanied children at the southwest border in the 12 months ending Sept. 30, up 77 percent from the previous year. More than 5,000 were then transferred to family members or other sponsors in New York City and on Long Island.

Alejandro and his younger brother Jeffrey, 13, were two of that number, picked up along the border in July, then placed on a plane by the federal Office of Refugee Resettlement. They were two boys who had grown into teenagers in one of the world's most dangerous environments, going to meet a father who had not seen them since they were little. Alejandro worried before the meeting, he said, speaking Spanish through an interpreter. "I didn't know if I would recognize him," he said of his father, even though they had communicated regularly by Skype.

For their father, Luis Rodriguez, 31, the arrival of his children at the border was both a danger and a gift — he had unlawfully come to the country around a decade ago and had avoided involvement with immigration officials. Now they had his name, address and phone number.

He, too, was anxious about the reunion. "My fear was that they weren't going to have that love for their father," he said, also speaking through an interpreter.

When Mr. Rodriguez saw Alejandro and his brother at the airport, he cried. "I felt their affection immediately," he said. "I felt in the hug that they needed me." He took risks by talking to Customs. But he said, "It was worth it because this will be our first Christmas together since he was 5."

Alejandro and Jeffrey were born in San Pedro Sula in northwestern Honduras, the country's second-largest city. Their mother was gone from their lives when they were quite young, and Mr. Rodriguez left for the United States when Alejandro was 5 or 6, planning to return after a few years. Even then, violence was a problem in San Pedro Sula, Mr. Rodriguez said.

It exploded after a 2009 military coup, as drug cartels and gangs waged open warfare in the streets. From 2011 to 2013, the city had the highest murder rate in the world, according to a Mexican research group, the Citizen Council for Public Safety and Criminal Justice (the group's study did not include the Middle East). Of the children detained by United States immigration agents, more come from San Pedro Sula than from any municipality in the world, according to the Pew Research Center — 2,200 from January to May alone.

In Honduras, Alejandro, living with his grandmother and missing his father, was left to watch over his younger brother. "He would ask why I had left, when I would return," Mr. Rodriguez said. "Sometimes

Alejandro Rodriguez in his neighborhood in Brooklyn.

on birthdays he would want me to be there. My only hope was that we would someday be together."

Guns were everywhere, and gangs pressed teenage boys into service; girls were raped or sold. "Men would stop us when we were on our way to school and go through our things," Alejandro said. Twice, gang members forced both boys from the bus, and several times they threatened Alejandro with guns, vowing to kill him if he did not join their gang, he said.

The boys asked their father to help them leave Honduras, but Mr. Rodriguez remembered his own trip north. He was beaten and robbed in Guatemala and Mexico, he said, at one point riding on the top of an infamous freight train known as the Beast. Mr. Rodriguez is a compact, genial man who smiles easily, but when he described his journey north, he stopped in tears.

"You could be assaulted, robbed or killed and left in the wild as if nothing happened," he said. "These are not things you want for your kids." Even as their lives in Honduras became more and more precarious, he told them not to come north.

Then on Mother's Day in 2011, armed men arrived on motorcycles at Alejandro's grandmother's house.

"Suddenly they stopped and opened fire without saying anything," Mr. Rodriguez said. "Alejandro and his brother ducked under a car in order to escape the bullets, but their uncle was killed." The gunmen told Alejandro and Jeffrey that if they went to the police, "they would have to face the consequences," Mr. Rodriguez said.

As his father spoke, Alejandro seemed to withdraw from the conversation, revealing no emotion. He is hard to read, often omitting or glossing over what are clearly horrific experiences.

Rebecca Press, a lawyer at Central American Legal Assistance who is representing Jeffrey (who declined to speak for this article) and Alejandro, said the boys' experience was typical among her clients. "The young people we come in contact with have been exposed to high levels of violence and been threatened themselves," she said. "There's a level of trauma that nobody seems to be dealing with."

Even in a town as violent as San Pedro Sula, the killing of children this spring was shocking. The children had been kidnapped, tortured and executed, probably for not cooperating with gangs. After that, the gangs stepped up their threats against Alejandro and his brother, Ms. Press said.

In early June, the boys saw a news program about American immigration officials' allowing unaccompanied minors into the country. The report was false, but the boys had no way of knowing that.

Two weeks later they left home, carrying a change of clothes, water and some food. Because of their father's opposition, they did not tell anyone they were leaving. Alejandro wore a knife on a chain under his shirt. They had 6,000 lempiras (about $283), which Alejandro divided among hiding places on his body.

On a series of buses, they crossed borders into Guatemala and then Mexico, meeting other travelers on the same route. Alejandro stayed

Alejandro, center, and his friend Carlos Castillo, right, at a Brooklyn N train station after school.

awake, keeping watch over his brother. For days they talked as little as possible, so that their accents would not give them away as foreigners.

Transfer points were the most dangerous. Three times they saw fellow passengers robbed or beaten by gangs, but no one bothered them. After the third robbery, near the United States border, they found a pay phone and called their father. "We told him that we were already in Mexico and could not turn back," Alejandro said.

Mr. Rodriguez had been frantic since learning the boys had left home five days earlier. "I was happy to hear from them but was also angry at the same time because of what they had done," he said.

By then they were part of a group of about six, the others all adults. The group crossed the Rio Grande into Texas by makeshift raft, just branches tied together with shoelaces. Their plan was to seek border agents on the other side, rather than risk wandering on their own in the June heat. "We thought we might get lost and never be seen again," Alejandro said.

They found agents soon enough, officers who had detained a group of migrants ahead of Alejandro's group. At an intake area, the agents gave them food and a change of clothes, and questioned them: Where were they from? How old were they? Why did they leave?

"I thought I was going to be sent back, because there was not a lot of space and a lot of people," Alejandro said. "If you have a bad attitude, you're sent back. We were very quiet." Then the agents asked the boys for their father's contact information.

Alejandro was vague about how long they were held in Texas. Maybe it was three days, maybe longer. Finally they were put on a 2 a.m. flight to La Guardia Airport.

In New York, there were adjustments to make. The streets and language were alien. Their father had started a new life, with a wife and a son; his apartment, a studio, was barely big enough for the three of them, let alone the addition of two adolescent boys. Mr. Rodriguez worked in an auto body shop, earning $800 a week — enough to support them, he said, since he had previously been sending money for the boys to Honduras. His wife, from El Salvador, stayed at home.

For many families, reunification comes with tension and recriminations. But if there are stresses in Alejandro's home, neither he nor his father let on.

The boys were directed to appear on Sept. 11 in Federal Immigration Court, part of an accelerated docket for minors that was created to discourage children from crossing the border. At the courthouse they were met by representatives of the city's Departments of Education and of Health and Mental Hygiene, who helped them enroll in school and in a free health insurance program. The Department of Homeland Security provided a list of free lawyers, including Ms. Press's group.

Ms. Press filed petitions for asylum, a process separate from Immigration Court, on Nov. 13. If the petitions are denied, the case will proceed in court.

On a rainy morning before Thanksgiving, the halls of Franklin Delano Roosevelt High School sang with polyglot chatter. Students there come from more than 50 countries, and 39 percent are classified as English-language learners, taking most of their classes in Spanish, Chinese or another language. Police officers monitor the halls, but there are no metal detectors for students to pass through. The school has a graduation rate slightly below the city average, but SAT scores are slightly higher. For Alejandro, who chose Roosevelt from a list of eight because he preferred a big school, this is his portal to his new life.

In algebra class, the teacher, Adnan Gomez, gave a word problem in English ("Julie lives four blocks east of F.D.R. and David lives four blocks west of F.D.R. …") while addressing the students mostly in Spanish.

Moments later, Alejandro raised his hand to solve a simple problem. When Mr. Gomez asked him to explain his reasoning, he did so in Spanish.

At Roosevelt, Alejandro was placed in relatively low-level classes, primarily because of his deficiency in English, said Steven DeMarco, the school's principal. Each day he has three classes in English as a second language. Alejandro said his grade point average was around 85. Mr. DeMarco said that teachers and guidance counselors watched students for signs of trauma, especially among recent arrivals from Central America — "changes in their personality or something they write" — but that they had not seen any signs so far. The school does not ask students their immigration status.

The city's Education Department does not keep track of how many recent undocumented immigrants have been added to the school system, or whether they have exhibited any effects from past traumas, said Milady Baez, senior executive director of its Department of English Language Learners and Student Support.

On Thursday, guidance counselors citywide began a training program with the Center for Child Trauma and Resilience at Mount Sinai

Beth Israel in response to the surge of unaccompanied minors. The training runs through June.

At school Alejandro plays on a soccer team with other recent immigrants. He made friends quickly, he said.

"We talk about how we arrived, how we're feeling, how was the trip," he said. "We all get sentimental."

But he still gets uncomfortable around English speakers. "When I get lost in conversation, I go on my cellphone so I don't feel awkward," he said. People on the street, he added, "would look at me and I didn't know if they were saying something bad about me." In a strange city, he found it hard to ask for directions, even from adults, because he did not know whether he could trust them.

After school one day, Alejandro and some Spanish-speaking friends were waiting for the subway, listening to music on a portable stereo, when another group of teenagers started yelling at them. "They said they didn't want to listen to music in Spanish," Alejandro said. The words escalated into blows; one boy was smashed into a metal garbage bin, bloodying his mouth.

Typical teenage stuff — but for Alejandro, it can be life-altering. Any serious trouble with the police or at school might endanger his immigration case. "You have divisions in the cafeteria, and fights between Chinese, Latin, Arab and black kids," Alejandro said. "They make fun of the way we speak, and the music."

Mr. Rodriguez said he had told Alejandro to keep his distance and to ask for help from teachers, security guards or police officers. "But he says, 'If I'm attacked, I will defend myself,' " Mr. Rodriguez said.

When father and son watched President Obama's prime-time speech last month announcing an executive order to grant temporary legal status for up to five million immigrants, their reaction was mixed.

Mr. Rodriguez can now live and work for three years without fear of deportation because his youngest child is an American citizen. But for Alejandro, the president's words changed nothing.

Still, he said his life had improved since he came north. He feels secure on the streets in a way that was impossible in Honduras. He has friends who are helping him learn English.

His lawyer, Ms. Press, said he was a good candidate for asylum, with a decision likely in early 2015. Though he does not neatly fit into the law's five eligibility groups — foreign nationals with a well-founded fear of persecution because of religion, race, nationality, political views or membership in a social group — asylum officers have interpreted the criteria broadly for minors, approving a much higher percentage of children than of adults. Because Alejandro witnessed his uncle's killing and because he lacked "effective familial protection," he could be considered part of an at-risk social group, Ms. Press said.

If that fails, she said, she will seek special immigrant juvenile status, for children who are abused, abandoned or neglected by one or both parents — in Alejandro's case, by his mother. Even with the accelerated docket, a final hearing on that application would probably be two years away, she said.

In the meantime, he has soccer, school and a budding romance — interests that were perilous in Honduras, not so scary here. He has the luxury of thinking about the future.

He said he would like to be a police officer, to be "protecting people and cruising around." That, too, was different from Honduras, where the police could be as dangerous as the gangs.

"Here you can serve calmly without fear of being killed," he said. It seemed like a dream to him. "But you need 60 college credits," he added, his spirit cooling at the thought.

He grinned a little bit. In time, that hurdle, too, might seem more manageable.

'No Asylum Here': Some Say U.S. Border Agents Rejected Them

BY CAITLIN DICKERSON AND MIRIAM JORDAN | MAY 3, 2017

TIJUANA, MEXICO — By the time Francisca, Armando and their two surviving children made it to the United States border in late February, they were hungry, exhausted and virtually penniless. But the couple, who said that a son had been killed by a gang back in El Salvador and that their daughter had nearly been raped, thought they had finally reached safety.

Under United States and international law, all people who ask for asylum are supposed to be allowed into the country to plead their case. But instead, they said, a Customs and Border Protection agent shooed them away.

"There is no asylum here," Francisca, 32, recalled the agent telling them. "We are not granting asylum."

Customs agents have increasingly turned away asylum seekers without so much as an interview, according to migrants and their lawyers, in a trend first noted several months ago and that appeared to accelerate after President Trump's inauguration. That has left an untold number of migrants trapped in Mexico, where they have sometimes fallen prey to kidnappers seeking ransom or been driven into the hands of drug cartels and smugglers. Some have tried to enter the United States illegally and dangerously, through the desert or across the Rio Grande, a risky journey.

"By rejecting asylum seekers at its borders, the United States is turning them away to face danger, persecution, torture, kidnappings and potential trafficking in Mexico," Human Rights First, an organization that has studied the problem, said in a report released on Wednesday.

No hard data exists on how often customs agents prevented asylum seekers from entering the United States, but many do make it past the border gates. Human Rights First said it had documented 125 people

Francisca, who requested her last name be withheld, said officials threatened to have her family deported if they did not retreat into Mexico.

or families from countries including Colombia, El Salvador, Guatemala, Mexico and Turkey who were turned away at entry points in Arizona, California and Texas from November to April. The organization said the actual number was likely to be far higher, since most of the migrants never make contact with a lawyer or an American advocate.

In response to questions, Customs and Border Protection said that the United States adhered to international law and convention permitting people to seek asylum on the grounds that they were being persecuted because of their race, religion, nationality, political belief or other factors.

"If an officer or agent encounters a U.S.-bound migrant without legal papers and the person expresses fear of being returned to his/her home country, our officers process them for an interview with an asylum officer," the agency said in a statement.

The Trump administration has not ordered customs agents to turn away asylum seekers. But the president has made it clear he believes the asylum system in its current form contributes to the problem of illegal immigration.

By law, those who request protection at a United States entry point must first be referred for a screening, known as a credible-fear interview, with an asylum officer from United States Citizenship and Immigration Services.

If the asylum officer decides people have a significant chance of proving a fear of persecution in their home country, they are allowed to apply for asylum before a judge, and from October 2016 through March 2017, according to the immigration agency, more than 38,000 people passed that step.

But in recent years, judges have approved less than half of asylum requests. For migrants from Mexico and Central American countries, those numbers are even lower: only 10 percent to 23 percent since 2011, according to data compiled by researchers at Syracuse University. Many asylum seekers from the region claim they have been targeted by gangs, which is harder to prove than political persecution, or base their claims on poverty, which is not a ground for asylum.

If they are denied, asylum seekers can be deported. But since many are released while their case is pending, some never return to court and evade deportation. The Trump administration has said asylum seekers should be released less often, and some lawyers said more of their clients are now being detained.

Border crossings have dropped drastically since Mr. Trump took office, a sign that his tough talk is discouraging people from even trying the journey. Advocates for migrants assert that Mr. Trump's talk has also emboldened some customs officers to ignore the law and take it upon themselves to keep migrants from receiving an asylum interview.

"The tenor of interactions with C.B.P. officers has veered toward the openly hostile following his election," said Nicole Ramos, an

American lawyer representing asylum seekers traveling through Tijuana.

Francisca, who requested her last name be withheld because of concerns for her family's safety, said she tried to show some documents to the border agent in Tijuana — the death certificate for their son who was killed and a police report documenting the attempted rape of their daughter, also by gang members. But the official threatened to have the family deported if they did not retreat into Mexico, she said.

"They treated us like we were trespassing," said Francisca, who returned to a shelter for women and children with her 14-year-old daughter. Her husband, Armando, is with their 18-year-old son at a men's shelter down the street.

The report by Human Rights First said that a Honduran family was kidnapped and forced to pay a ransom for their release after they were turned back to Mexico twice by agents in Texas. Shaw Drake, the lead researcher of the report, said the area surrounding the ports of entry in Texas had been nicknamed the "hunting ground," where cartels see migrants as easy prey for exploitation.

When he fled the Mexican state of Guerrero, Benito Jiménez Alarcón, 22, carried a plastic bag filled with photographs of injuries from the time he was kidnapped for three days by gang members. They show bruises spanning his back from side to side, where he said he was struck with clubs. His legs are covered in bright purple and blue knots from gun lashings.

He thought he would receive an asylum hearing after American border agents rifled through his belongings, including the photographs. The agents also asked him to remove his pants so they could see his injuries, he said.

But the agents, possibly acting beyond their purview, told him that he needed police reports. Mr. Jiménez, who was at a Tijuana shelter this week, said that it would be impossible to obtain such reports because the police and gangs in his village collaborate with each other.

A border agent told him he could claim asylum only with the help of a lawyer or through Grupo Beta, a Mexican organization that organized a numbering system to regulate the flow of migrants so they did not all seek asylum at once. But that system was intended mainly for Haitians, and non-Haitians have said they have not been given numbers.

Mary Galván, a Brazilian nun who runs Madre Assunta, a shelter for women and girls in Tijuana, said that asylum seekers who spend weeks preparing documents to prove their cases often return within hours because they are rebuffed at the border.

Outside in the courtyard, Abi and Cesia Quijada, 10- and 11-year-old girls from El Salvador, played with dolls and jewelry-making kits. Their mother, Sandra, spoke on the phone with her eldest daughter, Xiomara, 16, who was at a shelter in Texas. The family was separated in Mexico en route to Tijuana.

Sandra said she worried about Xiomara, who struggles with depression and has attempted suicide. "I feel so powerless," she said, explaining that they escaped together after Sandra's former partner, a gang member, became abusive.

Without looking up from the earrings she was carefully constructing with hot pink beads and purple plastic string, Cesia asked in Spanish if it was true that the United States was no longer accepting "refugios" — people seeking refuge — like them. Abi said she wanted to go to America "because it's safe there." Her sister added, "Because they protect children."

CAITLIN DICKERSON reported from Tijuana, and MIRIAM JORDAN from Los Angeles.

On the Border, a Discouraging New Message for Asylum Seekers: Wait

BY SIMON ROMERO AND MIRIAM JORDAN | JUNE 12, 2018

The Trump administration is determined to reduce the flow of asylum applicants coming into the United States. At some border crossings, migrants are being forced to wait for days or longer in Mexico.

NOGALES, MEXICO — In their monthlong odyssey taking them from violence-plagued El Salvador to the streets of this Mexican outpost on the Arizona border, the dream of finding protection in the United States somehow kept Carolina Cortez and her two children going.

But when they finally arrived in Nogales about two weeks ago and made their way to the fortified crossing where they planned to submit their request for asylum, the family's quest for safe haven was turned upside down by a dismaying new turn on the Mexican border, as the numbers of asylum seekers surge once again: They would have to wait.

"We've slept on the ground of Nogales since then," said Ms. Cortez, 36, alongside her 14-year-old daughter and 8-year-old son. "We fled a war zone dominated by gangs, walked across the desert, ran out of money," she added, describing their journey from the Salvadoran town of Olocuilta. "I have no idea what to do now but wait."

At an array of points along the United States-Mexico border, at lonely sentry boxes, remote bridges and crowded border crossings, the scenes over the past few weeks have been similar: desperate asylum seekers from Central America, many of them children, camped out on Mexican soil as they wait to apply for admission to the United States.

The growing number of Central American refugees sleeping near crossings on the border points to a resurgent exodus of people from countries grappling with gang violence, drug cartels and a lack of economic opportunities, as well as a shift in policies in the United States effectively making it harder for Central Americans to request asylum.

In a ruling on Monday, Attorney General Jeff Sessions said that immigration judges should not necessarily consider claims of domestic abuse or gang violence as a basis for asylum claims, absent other evidence that someone has suffered persecution as a member of a social group protected by law — a move that establishes a major new roadblock for thousands of Central Americans trying to seek refuge in the United States.

As word of the shift by Mr. Sessions spread on Monday to places on the border, a sense of even greater despair set in among some who have been sleeping near crossings.

"I'm sickened by a change like this since my country is a place where gangs extort money from innocents, and if you don't pay you get a shot in the head," said Yadira Barrios, 22, a maid from the city of San Pedro Sula in Honduras who has been camping out with her 4-year-old son, Marvin, near the border turnstiles in Nogales.

"The only thing I can do now is remind myself that our fate rests in God's hands," said Ms. Barrios, emphasizing that she is an evangelical Christian who attends a Pentecostal church. "I know there are also many people of faith in the United States. I hope they can pray for me and my son now."

But the Trump administration is also forcing significant numbers of asylum applicants to wait in Mexico before even submitting an application. Though there have been reports of asylum seekers being turned away since shortly after President Trump took office, the numbers appear to have climbed in recent weeks, with an unusually large number of applicants camped out near border crossings in California, Arizona and Texas.

Trump administration officials said Customs and Border Protection officials were taking a "proactive approach" to make sure only those with valid entry documents approached border stations, while those without legal documentation were being scheduled for processing as time permits.

"Depending upon port circumstances at the time of arrival, individuals presenting without documents may need to wait in Mexico as

CBP officers work to process those already within our facilities," an agency spokesman said in a statement.

"No one is being denied the opportunity to make a claim of credible fear or seek asylum," the spokesman added. "CBP officers allow more people into our facilities for processing once space becomes available or other factors allow for additional parties to arrive. This has been occurring intermittently as needed at several locations as well where the volume of arriving people exceeds the capacity of our facilities."

The spokesman said any delays are expected to be "temporary."

In downtown Nogales, near dentistry offices offering cut-rate root canals and pharmacies peddling Viagra prescription-free to American tourists, the bottleneck has produced a grim sight at the turnstiles where legally authorized border crossers step from Mexico into the United States.

Families from El Salvador, Guatemala and Honduras huddle together on the ground near packages of donated diapers and cans of baby formula. Some have endured this limbo for nearly two weeks, sleeping on the ground at night and trying to stay cool during the day as temperatures in this outpost in the Sonoran Desert surpass 100 degrees.

"We made it here on foot and by bus," said Justo Solval, 25, a laborer traveling with his 21-month-old son, Jonathan. They set out from Suchitepéquez in southwest Guatemala, escaping extortion gangs in an effort to request asylum in the United States, Mr. Solval said.

But after arriving in Nogales about a week and a half ago, they have been sleeping on cardboard pizza boxes in a squalid entryway to a bathroom at the border crossing.

"We depend on strangers for food, for water, for everything," Mr. Solval said. "I wanted to do everything legally, to ask for asylum in the proper way, but this is a setback I did not expect for us."

After a 44 percent decline in illegal entries during Mr. Trump's first year in office, the number of migrants showing up at the southwest border is on the rise again. Federal agents arrested nearly 52,000 people at the border in May, the third consecutive month of increase.

The latest data suggests that recent measures to crack down on illegal immigration have not deterred migrants, many of whom make the arduous journey over land from Central America to escape gangs and drug cartels, though others come in search of better jobs and education opportunities.

Some immigration experts argue that the asylum system in the United States is being abused by applicants who are seeking to move to the country primarily for economic reasons. But scholars who have examined the system closely say that the flow of asylum seekers from certain regions, especially the northern triangle of Central America, comprised of El Salvador, Guatemala and Honduras, reflects widespread human rights abuses in those countries.

"You always have to be careful of fraud, but having some economic motives for requesting asylum shouldn't necessarily be disqualifying," said Jaya Ramji-Nogales, a law professor at Temple University. "Widespread violence in some countries contributes to dire economic problems. Most people applying for asylum are fleeing a desperate situation."

The Trump administration in recent months deployed thousands of National Guard troops to the border, and on May 7 introduced a "zero-tolerance" policy that calls for prosecuting everyone who illegally enters the country.

Those who petition for asylum at official crossings like the one in Nogales are not considered illegal border-crossers, and are not prosecuted under that policy, yet their numbers are also so substantial that the Trump administration is struggling to control the influx.

Under current law, people who claim fear of persecution in their home countries are entitled to what is known as a credible fear interview. If they show a "significant possibility" of winning their asylum case, they are usually admitted into the United States to await a court hearing before a judge who decides their case.

Their cases join a ballooning backlog in the immigration courts, 700,000 in total, meaning they could take years to be decided, even though the Justice Department recently said it would set completion targets for judges.

Credible fear claims at the border soared 1,700 percent from 2008 to 2016, according to United States Citizenship and Immigration Services, whose officials conduct the interviews.

Across the country, only about 20 percent of all applicants were granted asylum in fiscal year 2017. That proves that people are making many claims without merit, administration officials contend.

"The asylum system is being abused to the detriment of the rule of law, sound public policy, and public safety — and to the detriment of people with just claims," Mr. Sessions said Monday. "Saying a few simple words — claiming a fear of return — is now transforming a straightforward arrest for illegal entry and immediate return into a prolonged legal process, where an alien may be released from custody into the United States and possibly never show up for an immigration hearing."

The government has been seeking to hold more migrants in detention to speed up their removal. It is also discouraging people from applying for asylum, immigrant advocates and lawyers say, by criminally prosecuting those applicants who enter the country illegally rather than letting them turn themselves in at an official border station. These people can only apply for asylum once their criminal case has been heard and they have served time.

Some migrants who have presented themselves at a port of entry to claim asylum have had their children taken from them, though that was only supposed to happen to those being prosecuted for illegally crossing the border, according to several immigrant advocacy organizations, as well as the American Civil Liberties Union, which is challenging such family separations in court.

In many cases, young people are making their way to the border alone to claim asylum — and they, too, are now facing delays and possible other roadblocks. Miguel Antonio Ayala, 16, a high school student from Honduras, arrived in Nogales recently and was among those camping out at the border crossing. He said he planned to request asylum in an effort to reunite with a sister living in Boston.

"My dream is to find work and attend university to study medicine," Mr. Ayala said. "I want to obey the laws of the United States and contribute to society. There's nothing for me in Honduras. I'd rather live on the streets of Nogales for a thousand days if it means not going back."

While some of the migrants have found beds in shelters in Nogales, others said they avoid the facilities out of fear of theft or abuse. Instead, they prefer to guard their spot on the asphalt so as not to lose their place in line when American officials at the crossing allow a handful each day to submit their asylum requests.

For those in Nogales who cross the border each day to work on the American side, the influx of Central Americans has become part of their routine in the slow-moving line at the crossing. Sometimes they need to step over families of migrants in order to present their documents.

"My heart goes out to these people because all they want is to provide for their children," said Aridaid Rodríguez, 21, who lives on the Mexican side of the border but works each day at a McDonald's restaurant on the American side. An American citizen, she said she was born in Phoenix but had to move to Mexico at the age of 9 when her Mexican-born mother was apprehended by immigration agents in Arizona and deported.

"Where's the dignity in treating families this way?" Ms. Rodríguez asked, referring not to her own saga but to that of the Central Americans sprawled out near the turnstiles. "No one should be forced to live like animals just to cross into the United States."

SIMON ROMERO is a national correspondent based in Albuquerque, covering immigration and other issues. He was previously the bureau chief in Brazil and in Caracas, Venezuela, and reported on the global energy industry from Houston.

MIRIAM JORDAN is a national immigration correspondent. She reports from a grassroots perspective on the impact of immigration policy. She has been a reporter in Mexico, Israel, Hong Kong, India and Brazil.

'We Are Full': What Asylum Seekers Are Told

OPINION | BY STEPHANIE LEUTERT AND SHAW DRAKE | JAN. 28, 2019

Families fleeing danger have been told to go to a U.S. port of entry, where border agents have been instructed to turn them away.

EVERY DAY, THE SAME SCENE plays out in the Mexican border city of Ciudad Juárez. Mixed into the flow of students, commuters and travelers are asylum-seeking families, arriving at their final destination, the entrance to the United States port of entry.

The families drop the required 4 pesos into the turnstile to begin their walk up the international bridge that arches over the Rio Grande and connects this part of Mexico to the United States. Yet when they reach the halfway point, demarcated by orange cones, Customs and Border Protection officers are waiting to turn them away from seeking safety in the United States — a right granted to them under American and international law.

Instead, these asylum-seeking families are provided with the same explanation: "We are full."

Conversations surrounding President Trump's focus on spending billions on a border wall have overshadowed border realities. For the past two years, as the number of asylum-seeking families and children has increased, the administration has ushered in a range of additional restrictive border policies. United States government officials have told migrants to go to ports of entry rather than crossing the border without authorization. However, simultaneously, they have imposed other policies that reject asylum seekers trying to do just that.

In July, a family of five arrived (navigating their way through Mexico with the help of smugglers) at the Eagle Pass-Piedras Negras border crossing to apply for asylum. The parents and their children — ages 12, 6, and 3 — had fled El Salvador after receiving targeted threats of violence from Barrio 18, a major gang in Central America.

The family approached border officers to assert their right to ask for asylum; they were also seeking help for a son who no longer had medicine for his chronic heart condition. In response, a border officer noted that he was not a doctor, physically pushed the family back across the international line into Mexico, and told them to return to Piedras Negras and the local migrant shelter there.

In the shelter, the family put their names on an informal waiting list for their chance to seek asylum again. However, their smugglers learned they had not yet entered the United States and began demanding more money, promising to infiltrate the shelter and kill the family if they did not send additional payments. Several days later, while the family walked to a convenience store, a white van screeched to a halt and armed men forced the family into the vehicle.

The family was taken to a house and spent two days in captivity, until Mexican state police arrived. However, these officers had not come to save the family but rather to sit down at the table for a leisurely breakfast and to accept money from the kidnappers. When the police did pay attention to the family, it was to call Mexican immigration agents to deport them. These agents proposed a deal, to release the family for $1,000. But with no more money, the family was transported to a Mexican migration detention center. After languishing for two months, the parents and children were released into Mexico City, where the threats continued both from their former kidnappers and Barrio 18 gang members searching for the family.

This family's harrowing story is far from an isolated case. In February 2017, a Honduran woman and her three children were kidnapped in the border city of Reynosa, Tamaulipas — the migrant kidnapping capital of Mexico — after trying to seek asylum with border officers on three occasions. And in November 2018, a transgender Mexican asylum seeker was robbed and assaulted in Tijuana. The next month, a Cameroonian asylum seeker was stabbed and two Honduran asylum-seeking teenagers were murdered.

Routine turnbacks and the expansion of "metering" systems at ports of entry began in 2016. Yet last summer, border officers doubled down on the practice, stationing its agents mid-bridge from El Paso to Brownsville and at border gates from New Mexico to San Diego with instructions to reject people seeking asylum. Today, these turnbacks are occurring daily at major ports of entry along the southwest border.

Asylum seekers who are denied entry to the United States must wait in Mexican migrant shelters or on the bridges themselves, vulnerable to a range of rights violations and safety concerns. This follows perilous journeys to escape violence at home to reach the United States and legally request protection.

The situation could be improved if United States officials allocated sufficient personnel and resources to efficiently process asylum seekers immediately upon their arrival to the border. However, the Trump administration has not taken these steps and has instead expanded metering and turnback policies. Just last week, the Department of Homeland Security announced it will implement a pilot initiative in California to return arriving asylum seekers to Mexico to await their eventual hearings before an immigration judge. Such a policy deliberately places thousands of people in situations similar to the young family of five that was kidnapped and extorted.

As violence and insecurity across Central America continues to go unaddressed, families will continue to join our border communities in search of protection for themselves and their children. Despite attempts to vilify and demonize them as political pawns, asylum seekers from around the world continue to see the promise of the United States. Seeking asylum is a right — one this country must uphold. It is not only the law, it is the moral imperative of this nation.

STEPHANIE LEUTERT is the director of the Mexico Security Initiative at the Robert S. Strauss Center for International Security and Law at the University of Texas at Austin. **SHAW DRAKE** is the policy counsel for the A.C.L.U. Border Rights Center.

With Trump's Tough Deterrents, Many Asylum Seekers on the Border Are Giving Up

BY JOSE A. DEL REAL, CAITLIN DICKERSON AND MIRIAM JORDAN | FEB. 16, 2019

TIJUANA, MEXICO — Pushed beyond their limits by prolonged waits in dangerous and squalid conditions in parts of Northern Mexico, thousands of caravan members who had been waiting to seek asylum in the United States appear to have given up, Mexican officials said, dealing President Trump an apparent win after a humbling week for his immigration agenda.

About 6,000 asylum seekers who had traveled en masse, many of them in defiance of Mr. Trump's demands that they turn around, arrived in Northern Mexico in late November as part of a caravan that originated in Honduras. Since then, more than 1,000 have accepted an offer to be returned home by the Mexican government, the officials said. Another 1,000 have decided to stay in Mexico, accepting work permits that were offered to them last fall, at the height of international consternation over how to deal with the growing presence of migrant caravans.

Mr. Trump resorted on Friday to declaring a national emergency after he failed to secure funding from Congress for a border wall that he said would block migrants from entering the United States. But the data from Mexican officials suggested that harsh policies he has introduced to crack down on asylum seekers may already be achieving some of its intended effects.

Added this week to new policies that are bearing down on asylum seekers — which include tight limits on the number of people who can apply for the status each day and a heightened standard of proof to qualify — was the extension of a rule that certain asylum seekers must wait in Mexico for the full duration of their legal cases, which can take years.

Natali, one of many Honduran migrants who is reconsidering her plan to seek asylum in the United States. For now, she has an apartment in Mexico.

The requirement originally applied only to adults, but the Department of Homeland Security expanded it to include families with children as well.

Among those who have been dissuaded, at least for now, is Natali, 32, who asked to be identified only by her first name because she feared for her safety. Speaking from her modest apartment atop a steep hill in western Tijuana, she explained that she and her husband had fled their home in El Progreso, Honduras, after she witnessed a murder carried out by a local criminal gang. Soon after, she began to receive threats in the mail warning her to keep quiet.

Once in Mexico, they heard about the increasingly long odds of receiving asylum in the United States, and feared more than anything that officials there would return them to their home country. Rather than crossing the border, they decided to seek humanitarian visas to remain in Mexico legally for at least one year, and have slowly begun to build a life.

She still believes she might ask for asylum in the United States, but is realistic about her chances. "I like Tijuana," she said. "It's a very pretty city and there's a lot of work." More than anything, she fears the United States would deport her back to Honduras.

Mexican officials said the data on people who have deferred or given up their quest for asylum in the United States reinforced an idea that is often raised by Mr. Trump: that many caravan members are not truly desperate for protection.

"What happened is that many people came on an adventure, trying their luck," said Cesar Palencia, Tijuana's chief of migrant services. "When they realized that it was hard to cross and the conditions in Mexico were also difficult, among many factors, they decided to return home."

The Honduran caravan ballooned in size as it swept through impoverished villages, drawing a swarm of national media attention and an eclectic mix of participants. Many came from poverty, lacking education and resources, and said they were unfamiliar with the complex set of laws that would ultimately determine who would be granted legal status in the United States, and who would not.

Immigrant advocates said that hype and false promises had attracted a group that was somewhat unrepresentative of typical asylum seekers. But they pointed to the roughly 4,000 members who had successfully entered the United States and had at least requested protected status to argue that most had legitimate claims.

Michelle Brané, the director of migrant rights and justice at the Women's Refugee Commission, warned that while Mr. Trump's tough policies may discourage the undeserving, they might also endanger people who need protection. She said they would likely drive vulnerable migrants into the arms of human traffickers, who promise to provide passage into the United States.

"It may look like it's working in the short term," Ms. Brané said, "But I don't think it's a long-term solution. It's driving people further into the shadows and that's exactly the opposite of what we want."

When they arrived in Mexico, many of the caravan members had been living in squalor, sleeping in tents or lean-tos inside the Benito Juárez sports complex. A downpour devastated the grounds, and those who remained fled to a new expansive shelter called Barretal on the outskirts of Tijuana. Once packed with 2,500 people, that location also recently closed because it had shrunk to fewer than 200.

"It is not the same as when we had Barretal and Benito Juárez," said Esme Flores, an immigrant-rights advocate at the San Diego office of the American Civil Liberties Union. "It really feels that the population has moved on."

On Friday, all that remained of the formerly bustling migrant quarter around the Barretal shelter was a small camp around the corner, only partially covered by a tin roof. The conditions are far from comfortable, but the occupants said it was better than sleeping on sidewalks.

Most were not yet ready to give up trying to enter the United States, but knew of others who had. Elde Rodriguez, 26, said he had left Honduras hoping to send money back to his wife and daughter. Believing that he would not qualify for asylum, he tried last week to cross the border illegally but he and a friend were unable to find their away across and turned back.

"There's enough work here in Mexico, and you can live on that if you're alone. But you can't make enough to send money home, and that's the point about all this," he said. "If I can't get in, I'll just keep trying."

While Tijuana appears to be emptying, large groups of migrants have accumulated in other areas along the border as a result of the new policies. After a riot the day before, authorities in Mexico said on Friday that they would disband a group of 1,400 Central American asylum seekers who had been waiting in the city of Piedras Negras to cross the border into Eagle Pass, Tex., according to news reports.

The Trump administration has said that the latest policy requiring asylum seekers to wait in Mexico, which it called Migrant Protection

Protocols, is a vital response to a crisis at the border. Kirstjen Nielsen, secretary of the Department of Homeland Security, has said the policy aims to alleviate a humanitarian crisis on the border and secure the United States. Introduced as a pilot program across the border from San Diego, the administration plans to expand the policy into Texas.

Border Patrol apprehensions of families along the southwest border remain near all-time highs, though there was a slight downward turn in January, as is often the case, according the latest government figures. Customs and Border Protection said more than 1,800 Central American parents and children crossed the border illegally on Monday, the largest number of families recorded on a single day. And like other asylum policies of this administration, the "remain in Mexico" policy has already drawn legal scrutiny, leaving its future uncertain.

On Thursday, the American Civil Liberties Union and two other groups sued the administration on behalf of 11 asylum seekers who were required to wait in Mexico, claiming that the policy, which was introduced last month at the San Ysidro port of entry, near San Diego, violates United States and international laws.

The lawsuit was filed in federal court in the Northern District of California on behalf of migrants from Guatemala, Honduras and El Salvador who feared for their lives in Mexico, according to the complaint.

One of them was robbed at gunpoint and told by the assailant that he would be killed if he was seen again. Two others said that they had been threatened by local residents wielding rocks or sticks. Another plaintiff said he had to bribe a police officer to avoid arrest.

"Asylum seekers in Mexico face a heightened risk of kidnapping, disappearance, trafficking, sexual assault and murder, among other harms," said the complaint.

In December, the A.C.L.U. successfully sued the administration over another new rule that became known as the "asylum ban" because it significantly restricted the locations where people could request the status. That policy remains enjoined by a federal court; the Supreme Court declined to reinstate it.

Like members of the caravan, many of those who continue to come to the United States each day lack a comprehensive understanding of the system they are entering.

Ela Marina Rodriguez, 49, and her daughter, Duña Ventura, 16, arrived in Tijuana about three weeks ago and were taken to the small shelter by a man whom they had been traveling with. Ms. Rodriguez said she had heard on the news that bringing her daughter would guarantee them admission into the United States, and the two thought if they could make it through the journey they would have an opportunity for a better life.

"That's why we came all this way," she said. "I've dreamed of doing this my entire life but I was afraid. Hiding through the desert and the mountains, I never had the courage before, until we heard they were giving papers to families."

Her eyes grew wide when she heard from a reporter that some asylum seekers are being made to wait in Mexico. She sighed heavily and replied: "I don't know. I don't know. I don't want to be here."

Ms. Rodriguez said that "honestly, yes" she would cross illegally if that is what it takes to get into the United States. But if she is unable to gain entry to the United States, she said, she would likely turn back to Honduras. "I mean, what else can you do in that case?"

Waiting for Asylum in the United States, Migrants Live in Fear in Mexico

BY ZOLAN KANNO-YOUNGS AND MAYA AVERBUCH | APRIL 5, 2019

TIJUANA, MEXICO — Hoping to convince American immigration officials that his life is in danger, Selvin Alvarado sorted through photographs of men who he said have threatened to kill him.

Mr. Alvarado said he fled Honduras last fall after exposing corruption in his hometown and was followed into Mexico by an armed group. Once he reached the United States, he believed he would be safe — even if that meant being detained while waiting for asylum.

"I prefer 1,000 times being jailed," he said last week at a shelter south of the United States border, "than being dead."

Instead, as part of a newly expanded Trump administration policy, Mr. Alvarado, 29, a father of two, was sent back to Mexico. He has been waiting for weeks to be summoned for an asylum hearing in California.

Hundreds of asylum seekers are expected to be blocked from waiting in the United States each day under the so-called Remain in Mexico policy, which American officials describe as a deterrent to illegal immigration.

Officials at the Department of Homeland Security said the policy also aims to ease overcrowded detention facilities as they grapple with a recent surge in migrants along the southwestern border. The policy is being challenged in federal court.

"The crisis at our border is worsening, and D.H.S. will do everything in its power to end it," Kirstjen Nielsen, the homeland security secretary, said this week.

On Thursday, an official from Mexico's Foreign Ministry said it was unclear how many asylum seekers might be turned away from the United States under the policy, which he said the Trump administration had expanded without its consultation. The official spoke on the condition of anonymity to discuss a delicate diplomatic issue.

Daniela Diaz, 19, who said she was threatened with rape and death by a gang in El Salvador, is living in a shelter in Tijuana as American courts consider her asylum application.

About 633 Central American asylum seekers have been turned away since January, unable to prove sufficient fear of being tortured and persecuted in Mexico. It is a shift from earlier guidelines, which allowed migrants who convinced the authorities that they had a credible fear of returning to their home nations to remain in the United States while their asylum cases were being considered.

Stories of fleeing violence, extortion and corruption in their home countries do not meet the new standard for entry. Many migrants are also unable to obtain lawyers to represent them in court without first meeting them in the United States.

Mr. Alvarado said he was considering sneaking into the United States if his asylum claim was further delayed.

"I'll have to do it illegally," Mr. Alvarado said, holding photographs of the men who he said pursued him from Honduras, through Guatemala and into Tapachula, Mexico. "I'll have to give up everything."

For the most part, the policy has been rolled out slowly and quietly.

When it began at the San Ysidro port of entry in California in late January, only men traveling by themselves from Central America were told to wait in Mexico as their asylum cases wound through the American legal system. The policy has since expanded to stop entire families from waiting in the United States, although unaccompanied children and Mexican citizens will be allowed to enter.

It is now being enforced at border ports at Calexico, Calif., where President Trump traveled on Friday to tour the border, and El Paso. Ms. Nielsen has directed her department to expand the policy to other legal crossing points from Mexico.

The number of border crossings are nowhere as high as in the early 2000s, when as many as 220,000 migrants crossed the border in a month. Ms. Nielsen estimated last month that border officials had stopped as many as 100,000 migrants in March, up from 76,000 in February.

A State Department report released last month acknowledged the possibility that the migrants were no safer in Mexico from the same gangs that threatened them in Central America than they had been at home.

That is constantly on the mind of Daniel Nuñez, who was working as a security guard in Honduras when gang members opened fire in October, severely injuring several of his colleagues.

Mr. Nuñez fled to the United States border, where he asked for asylum in Calexico, but he was recently sent back to the Mexican city of Mexicali to wait for his immigration hearing.

The closest American immigration court is 30 minutes away. But Mr. Nuñez was told he had to report for his hearing at the San Ysidro port, a nearly three-hour drive.

He has no car, is sleeping in a shelter with about 370 other people and is trying to figure out how to get to San Ysidro. "I was thinking about that," he said last week, scratching his head. "How I was going to manage."

In a lawsuit filed in February in federal court in San Francisco, the American Civil Liberties Union accused the government of violating immigration law by returning asylum seekers to Mexico. The Trump

A dormitory at a migrant shelter in Mexicali. "You have to understand that they are shelters, not hotels, and there's no city, no state, that has sufficient resources to prepare for this," said Gustavo Magallanes Cortés, the director of migration affairs for Baja California.

administration has maintained it has broad discretion over removal proceedings.

Jacqueline Brown Scott, a lawyer, represents one of the plaintiffs in the case, who is identified in court papers only as Howard Doe for protection. He claims to have fled a drug cartel in Honduras, only to be kidnapped by another cartel in Mexico. He escaped after 15 days and he went to the United States border to seek asylum.

Immigration authorities diverted him to Tijuana. Last week, he appeared in immigration court in San Diego, where Ms. Scott argued that he had a fear of persecution in Mexico. He was sent back again.

"I told them everything, but they didn't seem to care," the migrant said in a text message that was viewed by The New York Times, which is withholding his name for security concerns.

Some migrants face additional delays from immigration judges who insist they find legal counsel before their cases can move forward.

Denis Rostran, of Honduras, said he called 10 lawyers who were listed on a document that Department of Homeland Security officials gave to him when he was sent back to Tijuana. None answered. Mr. Rostran said he has slept some nights on the street and has been robbed twice.

A Department of Homeland Security official said it was committed to ensuring migrants have legal assistance at no cost to the government. The agency also is not forcing migrants to return to Mexico who would "more likely than not" be persecuted or tortured there, the official said.

Twenty shelters and churches in Tijuana are housing around 3,000 migrants — and have almost reached their limit, said Esmeralda Siu, the executive coordinator of the Migrant Defense Coalition, in the Mexican state of Baja California. Many of the migrants are awaiting their court dates, she said, and do not expect to leave soon.

That means that newly arrived and future migrants will have few, if any, options for shelter.

"There's no city, no state, that has sufficient resources to prepare for this," said Gustavo Magallanes Cortés, the director of migration affairs for Baja California. "They've allowed these people to return, but cut the resources for migrants, which has led to chaos. Every day a shelter calls me and says, 'I've run out of food.'"

But many of the waiting migrants are determined to keep hope.

"Many people say they're doing this just so we get tired and give up on our cases," said Daniela Diaz, 19, who said she left El Salvador after a member of the MS-13 gang threatened to rape and kill her. She has been living in a shelter in Tijuana since late January.

She is frustrated that following the rules and asking for asylum at a legal port of entry — instead of sneaking into the United States — have resulted in a system of immigration purgatory.

"There's a lot of people throwing themselves over the wall," Ms. Diaz said, "and we're doing this the fair way."

AZAM AHMED contributed reporting from Mexico City.

'I Don't Want to Die': Asylum Seekers, Once in Limbo, Face Deportation Under Trump

BY CHRISTINA GOLDBAUM | APRIL 21, 2019

INDRA SIHOTANG WAS DESPERATE to stay in New York. Minutes from being deported to Indonesia, the 52-year-old father clung to a chair bolted to the floor at Kennedy International Airport, struggling against four immigration officers trying to tear him away.

By the end of the confrontation, his face was bloody and bruised. But neither Mr. Sihotang, nor another immigrant in the officers' custody who watched the incident unfold, was allowed onto the plane after the pilot raised security concerns.

"I kept trying to explain to them that the conditions in my country are very bad now," Mr. Sihotang said. "I was telling them, 'I don't want to die there.' "

Mr. Sihotang had lost his fight to receive asylum in the United States a decade ago, a decision he did not appeal after he and thousands like him were granted a temporary reprieve from deportation by the Obama administration. Days after assuming office, President Trump revoked that protection, making Mr. Sihotang and thousands of other asylum seekers suddenly eligible for deportation, though many did not realize it.

Even as Mr. Trump has sought in recent days to limit who can apply for asylum, and to expand indefinite detention for asylum seekers, his administration has with little public notice been carrying out a crackdown on people who asked for asylum, did not receive it and remained in the United States.

The policy, which often involves seeking out immigrants who have been in the country for years in a legal gray area, shows how the Trump administration aims to reverse what it believes are the misguided policies of the Obama administration.

Indra Sihotang, 52, with his wife and their children in their Queens home. Mr. Sihotang, an asylum seeker, was granted a temporary reprieve from deportation by the Obama administration. President Trump revoked that safeguard.

Immigration agents have been especially active in New York City. Deportations of immigrants with no criminal convictions, including asylum seekers with years- or decades-old deportation orders, rose to 1,144 in the 2018 federal fiscal year from 313 in 2016, a 266 percent increase, according to a recent report from the city comptroller.

That is the largest percentage increase of any Immigration and Customs Enforcement field office in the country.

The Trump administration said ICE agents are following the law in trying to return asylum seekers who have lost their cases on the merits and have no right to remain in the country.

But as these people are caught in a deportation dragnet, they risk being sent to countries where the persecution threats they face are even greater than when they fled to the United States, asylum seekers and lawyers say.

In the final years of the Obama administration, immigration judges were instructed to use prosecutorial discretion to grant some undocumented immigrants, such as asylum seekers who had lost their cases, the ability to stay and work in the United States legally as long as they regularly checked in with ICE.

These enforcement policies were designed to focus ICE's limited resources on deporting unauthorized immigrants who had criminal convictions, recently crossed the border or posed a threat to national security.

Until Mr. Trump came into office, asylum seekers like Mr. Sihotang "had no reason to try to reopen their asylum case because they were permitted to stay and work in this country," Amber Gracia, an immigration lawyer in Texas, said. "When the government suddenly seeks removal, these people are caught off guard."

She questioned why agents were focusing on deporting undocumented immigrants who had not broken the law, rather than focusing on violent criminals in the country illegally.

ICE officials said that as long as there was a standing deportation order for an individual, there would be legal grounds to take that person into custody.

"The U.S. government provides all those in removal proceedings with an opportunity to apply and be considered for relief from removal," an ICE spokeswoman, Rachael Yong Yow, said in a statement. "If an immigration judge finds an individual ineligible for any form of relief, the judge will issue a final order of removal, which ICE carries out in accordance with applicable U.S. law."

She said she could not comment on specific cases.

After losing his original asylum case five years ago, Mr. Sihotang lived and worked legally in New York City and watched as the persecution of Christians like him intensified in Indonesia.

When he arrived for his biannual check-in with ICE — a condition of his reprieve — in summer 2017, he said he had thought that it would proceed like every other: He would update his home address, provide his work address and confirm that he had not been arrested or convicted of a crime.

But this time, the ICE officer asked him to renew his passport and return to the ICE office. When he returned with the new passport, ICE took him into custody.

Only when ICE drove him to Kennedy Airport four weeks later did Mr. Sihotang realize why the ICE officer had requested that he renew his passport: The plan was to put him on a commercial flight to Indonesia.

"I was shocked," Mr. Sihotang said. "I was thinking about my kids. I told them, 'I've got four kids and my family. How will they survive without me?' "

Months after the confrontation at the boarding gate last year, ICE again tried to deport Mr. Sihotang. But this time, as he sat in a van minutes away from the airport, an ICE officer received a call telling him to stop the deportation.

A judge had determined Mr. Sihotang faced credible fears of persecution in Indonesia and reopened his asylum case, which remains unresolved.

The asylum seeker who watched Mr. Sihotang's first airport confrontation requested that he be identified only by his nickname, Neo, and that his home country not be named for fear of persecution. He was deported from New York weeks after that encounter, despite last-minute attempts to reopen his asylum case.

"I didn't do anything criminal," Neo said, breaking into tears. "I didn't do anything wrong, then suddenly they just sent me back."

One aspect of Neo's asylum case, he and his lawyer said, was a medical condition he had developed for which he needed daily medication unavailable in his home country. When he boarded his deportation flight to East Asia, he said he had three weeks' worth of the medication left. So, he said, he started to ration it: Take one pill. Skip a day. Take another.

"I was worried I was going to die," he said.

His only hope was his lawyer in the United States, who had filed an appeal to the Board of Immigration Appeals, the highest immigration court in the country.

The board determines whether an asylum seeker's claim has new merits and can issue an order preventing ICE from deporting an immigrant while that decision is made.

Since Mr. Trump came into office, more immigrants are making requests to the board to temporarily prevent a deportation.

But the denial rate for those requests has sharply increased, according to analysis by the Benjamin N. Cardozo School of Law in New York.

Steven Stafford, a spokesman for the Justice Department, said judges on the board "apply the law to the facts of the case before them."

When the board grants these requests, it is often only hours before an immigrant is scheduled to board a deportation flight, lawyers say. Some asylum seekers have even had their cases reopened after they have been deported.

Last spring, Neo was brought back to the United States by ICE after the board agreed to reopen his asylum case.

Still, not everyone is as lucky.

Immigration lawyers pointed to the circumstances of a Bangladeshi man who requested that he be identified only by his given name, Mahbub, because of an unresolved asylum case. He was granted permission to stay in the United States until the board reconsidered his case. He had sought asylum on the grounds that he was being persecuted over his political affiliation.

But the panel's decision, which arrived in his lawyer's inbox at 9 a.m., came four hours too late: At 5 a.m., he had been put on a flight to Bangladesh.

When he arrived in the Bangladeshi capital, Dhaka, he said he called his mother who, distraught, told him that he could not come to their home. One of his friends in the opposition party, in which Mahbub was an activist, had been arrested in the months before his return.

Fearing he faced the same fate, Mahbub, 36, said that he went into hiding. Months later, he paid a smuggler to help make his way to France, where he sought asylum.

"I'm just happy I stayed alive," Mahbub said.

'Every Day I Fear': Asylum Seekers Await Their Fate in a Clogged System

BY MIRIAM JORDAN AND JOSE A. DEL REAL | MAY 1, 2019

President Trump wants to discourage asylum claims, as immigration courts deal with a backlog of more than 800,000 cases. Here are four of them.

THEY TRAVELED THOUSANDS of miles and endured dangerous — and at times unimaginable — conditions on their journeys. They fled domestic violence, vengeful gangs, political opposition and laws that made their lives unbearable.

In droves, migrants have arrived at the United States' southern border claiming to have fled oppressive conditions in their home countries. Today, more than 800,000 await proceedings that could put them on the path to American citizenship.

But in a memo this week intended to discourage migrants — most of whom began their treks in Central America — President Trump ordered sweeping changes to the asylum process, an already byzantine system in which asylum seekers often wait years for their cases to be adjudicated because of a bottleneck in the immigration courts.

Among the directives: Asylum seekers would have to pay a fee to apply. And those who entered the country illegally would be barred from receiving work permits while their cases were adjudicated, which Mr. Trump said must happen within 180 days.

It could be months before the measures, which are likely to face legal challenges, take effect. Although only a small number of applicants ultimately win asylum, the orders could hurt those with legitimate claims, said critics of the directives.

We asked four people who are awaiting asylum hearings about their cases, and how they have fared in the United States.

CALLAGHAN O'HARE FOR THE NEW YORK TIMES

Asylum seekers at the bus station in San Antonio.

'I CRIED OF JOY.'

Name, age, country: Wendy, 27, El Salvador

Asylum claim: Wendy said she and her son were sexually assaulted by gang members in retaliation for her brother's cooperation with law enforcement.

Time in the United States: Three years

Work permit: Yes

In 2015, Wendy fled to the United States with her three children, including her 2-month-old daughter; she said she and her oldest child had been tied up and raped by gangs.

Wendy had to undergo reconstructive anal surgery, she said, and her son, who was 8 at the time, was severely traumatized. He continues to suffer from psychotic episodes and depression, which have led him to engage in acts of self-harm, she said. His hand bears scars from cutting himself with a plastic soda bottle.

In February, an immigration judge approved her asylum case,

pending the completion of a biometric examination. Once her case is finalized, Wendy and her three children will be eligible for permanent legal residency in the United States.

"Oh my God, I cried of joy. I felt so happy. I felt grateful," said Wendy, who asked that neither her last name nor her son's name be published, for fear that her family could face retribution from MS-13 gang members. "We would die if we were forced to return to El Salvador. We had the need for protection from this country."

According to current immigration regulations, asylum seekers are entitled to legally work in the United States once their asylum application has been pending for 180 days.

Wendy, who packs fruits and vegetables, said that working while her case was under review has meant feeding her family, paying rent and affording medication for her son.

Wendy's lawyer, Eileen Blessinger, said that many of her clients would have to rely on friends, family and charity if they were prohibited from working. Lack of income poses barriers to retaining a lawyer and obtaining a driver's license, and it compels people to work in the underground economy, she said.

'I AM VERY DISTRESSED.'

Name, age, country: Mamadou, 41, Guinea

Asylum claim: Mamadou was a high-profile activist who was targeted by the opposition party in his country, and whose family endured violence as a result of his political opinions.

Time in the United States: Five years

Work permit: Yes

Government soldiers in Guinea who were determined to capture Mamadou poured scalding oil on his baby when they came searching for him in his family's home in 2015, he claimed. Mamadou was already in the United States, where he had applied for asylum.

If the activist, who lives in the Bronx, wins his case, his family can join him. But three years later, his case has not yet been reviewed by a judge.

"Every second, every day I fear for the safety of my child and wife," said Mamadou, who asked that his last name be withheld out of concern for his family. "I am very distressed. So much time has already passed, and the situation in my country is only getting worst."

His lawyer, Carmen Maria Rey, is confident that her client has a strong claim, if only it would be adjudicatcd.

'IT BECAME JUST A NIGHTMARE.'

Name, age and country: Denis Davydov, 32, Russia

Asylum claim: Mr. Davydov, who is gay and H.I.V. positive, left his country because L.G.B.T. individuals face increasingly harsh treatment there.

Time in the United States: Four and a half years

Work permit: Yes

Mr. Davydov, who is living in San Jose, Calif., has been waiting since the spring of 2015 for his asylum case to be heard. Two years ago, he was detained by customs agents who believed he had overstayed his visa. He was held in detention in Miami for 45 days before he was released. His next hearing is scheduled for July.

He said being an L.G.B.T. individual in Russia put him at risk of increasingly harsh treatment, from everyday discrimination on the street to threats and beatings. He said he had also struggled to receive adequate treatment for his illness.

"I was told in a clinic they could not give me any medication because they didn't have them. It was the last straw. It was devastating," he said. "As a teenager, I was always questioned and bullied for being gay. And I was beaten. But all these laws started coming in. Before you could hide, but now, everywhere, it is the most popular topic. It became just a nightmare."

Today, Mr. Davydov works as a certified sommelier.

"It makes me so happy," he said. "It is my dream."

'I WOULD BE GOING HUNGRY.'

Name, age, country: Maria Meza, 40, Honduras

Asylum claim: Violence against her family.

Time in the United States: Four months

Work permit: No

Maria Meza was seeking a safe haven from gang violence in Honduras when she decided to journey north with a migrant caravan to Tijuana, Mexico, late last year.

In December, Ms. Meza and two of her daughters were among hundreds of asylum seekers who were tear gassed by the Border Patrol as they approached the border. Officials said that the officers fired tear gas because the migrants were mounting an assault.

A photograph of Ms. Meza and her children fleeing plumes of tear gas went viral. Ultimately, she and her children were allowed to enter the United States through a port of entry at Otay Mesa, Calif., where they requested protection in the United States with the assistance of lawyers and members of Congress.

Immigration authorities fitted Ms. Meza with an ankle monitor to track her movements and issued her a notice to appear in court — on a date that has not been scheduled — so that she could formally request asylum.

She has been reporting every two weeks to Immigration and Customs Enforcement as required. However, until her case is filed with the court, she is not eligible for a work permit.

"I ask God to give me an opportunity for asylum," she said in an interview. While she waits, churches, synagogues and community organizations have provided her with financial assistance. "Without the support of all these people, I would be going hungry."

MIRIAM JORDAN is a national immigration correspondent. She reports from a grassroots perspective on the impact of immigration policy. She has been a reporter in Mexico, Israel, Hong Kong, India and Brazil.

A New Migrant Surge at the Border, This One From Central Africa

BY MANNY FERNANDEZ | JUNE 16, 2019

SAN ANTONIO — For months, a migrant-services center blocks from the Alamo in downtown San Antonio has been packed with Central American families who have crossed the border in record-breaking numbers.

But in recent days, hundreds of migrants from another part of the world have caused city officials already busy with one immigrant surge to scramble on a new and unexpected one. Men, women and children from central Africa — mostly from the Democratic Republic of Congo and Angola — are showing up at the United States' southwest border after embarking on a dangerous, monthslong journey.

Their arrival at the border and at two cities more than 2,100 miles apart — San Antonio and Portland, Me. — has surprised and puzzled immigration authorities and overwhelmed local officials and nonprofit groups. The surge has prompted Portland to turn its basketball arena into an emergency shelter and depleted assistance funds meant for other groups. Officials in both cities have had to reassure the public that fears of an Ebola outbreak were unfounded while also pleading for volunteer interpreters who speak French and Portuguese.

In San Antonio, the city-run Migrant Resource Center has assisted about 300 African migrants who were apprehended at the border and released by the authorities since June 4. Those 300 are just a portion of the overall numbers. Since October 2018, more than 700 migrants from Africa have been apprehended at what has become their main point of entry, the Border Patrol's Del Rio sector, a largely rural stretch of Texas border that is nearly 200 miles west of San Antonio.

Migrants from around the world have been known to cross the southwest border, but the vast majority are those from Guatemala, Honduras, El Salvador and Mexico. African migrants have shown up at the border in the past, but only in small numbers, making the sudden

Migrants lining up for a meal inside a shelter in San Antonio. A surge of migrants from Central Africa has left officials scrambling to respond.

arrival of more than 700 all the more surprising to Border Patrol officials. From fiscal years 2007 to 2018, a total of 25 migrants from Congo and Angola were arrested and taken into custody in the Border Patrol's nine sectors on the southern border, according to agency data.

Many come with horrific stories of government-sanctioned violence at home and treacherous conditions on their long journeys through South and Central America.

"It's definitely an anomaly that we have not experienced before," said Raul L. Ortiz, the Border Patrol's chief patrol agent for the Del Rio sector. "We do know there are some more in the pipeline. We're going to prepare as if we should expect more."

In both San Antonio and Portland, elected officials, volunteers and nonprofit and religious leaders have rallied to assist the African migrants, donating money, serving free meals and operating overnight shelters. But their resources were already being stretched thin, and there was frustration among local officials about the federal government's handling of the African migrant surge.

Many of the Central American asylum seekers apprehended at the border have solidified their travel plans by the time they are released by Border Patrol or Immigration and Customs Enforcement. The migrants arrange to travel by plane or bus to join relatives already living in the United States.

But many of the recent African migrants do not have relatives in the country, so they are being released with no travel arrangements, a problem that local officials and nonprofit groups are forced to sort out. Some of the Congolese migrants in San Antonio said Border Patrol agents had chosen their destination cities for them, or encouraged them to select one of two cities, New York and Portland.

A Border Patrol spokesman denied those claims, saying the agency is not directing migrants toward any particular destination.

In Portland — the largest city in Maine, with a population of 66,417 — about 200 African migrants were sleeping on cots on Friday night in a temporary emergency shelter set up in the Portland Expo Center. The city has a large Congolese community, and has built a reputation as a place friendly to asylum seekers. It created the government-financed Portland Community Support Fund to provide rental payments to landlords and other forms of assistance for asylum seekers, the only fund of its kind in the country, Portland officials said.

The mayor of Portland, Ethan K. Strimling, said they welcomed African migrants, and a donation campaign for them had raised more than $20,000 in its first 36 hours.

"I don't consider it a crisis, in the sense that it is going to be detrimental to our city," Mr. Strimling said. "We're not building walls. We're not trying to stop people. In Maine, and Portland in particular, we've been built on the backs of immigrants for 200 years, and this is just the current wave that's arriving."

San Antonio officials said they had sent about 150 of the roughly 300 African migrants in the city to Portland. The others traveled to

Chicago, Dallas, Denver, New York City, and cities in Florida and Iowa. Catholic Charities of San Antonio spent about $125,000 on airfare and bus tickets for African migrants in recent days, draining the funding it had planned on using to assist Central American migrants. Meanwhile, the $200,000 Portland government-assistance fund was already overextended by $90,000.

"No one has been prepared for anything like this," said J. Antonio Fernandez, the president and chief executive of Catholic Charities of San Antonio. "We were thinking that we were going to spend $120,000 in three to four months. We spent everything in five days. We're going to need help from people out there who want to help immigrants."

On Friday, the migrant center — a former Quiznos sandwich shop in a city-owned building, across the street from the downtown bus station — was filled with about 100 migrants, roughly 30 of whom were from Congo and Angola, and the rest from Central America. Outside, African families stood talking in groups or sat on the sidewalk with their backs against the wall.

They did not hide their anguish or their tears. The Congolese spoke of fleeing violent clashes between militia fighters and government soldiers, widespread corruption and government-led killings. Some of them traveled to the neighboring country of Angola, then flew to Ecuador. From there, they said they had traveled by bus and on foot through Colombia, Panama, Costa Rica, Nicaragua, Honduras, Guatemala and Mexico to the South Texas border.

One Congolese woman cried as she stood on the sidewalk. She said her 5-year-old daughter had gotten sick and died on a bus. "There weren't any doctors, there wasn't any medicine," she said. "It's too hard for me to talk about my story."

A 41-year-old man from Congo's capital, Kinshasa, said he and his 10-year-old son had spent four months traveling to the border with a group of about 10 families. The man, a Red Cross volunteer and mechanic who asked to be identified only by his first name, Alain, said he fled because he had been speaking out about government killings.

"I cannot go back now," Alain said. "They will kill me. We prefer to live in freedom. In my country there's no freedom, no democracy. We're cornered. We're prisoners in our own country."

The most treacherous part of the journey for many of the Congolese was in the Darién Gap, a region of mountains, forest and swampland at the border between Panama and Colombia that is considered one of the world's most dangerous jungles, where smugglers and armed criminals prey on migrants.

Alain said he was robbed at gunpoint there. A Congolese woman, sitting on the sidewalk outside the center, said in tears that she was raped in the Darién Gap jungle.

The woman, Gisele Nzenza Kitandi, 44, said migrants there had died because they were sick or dehydrated. Ms. Kitandi grew increasingly distraught, as she sat with her leg in a brace from being shot by Congolese government soldiers. She said she had no money for bus tickets for her and her children.

"I don't even have one dollar," Ms. Kitandi said.

Dr. Colleen Bridger, the interim assistant city manager of San Antonio, said the city would figure out a way to get the Africans the services and transportation they needed. The city and nonprofit groups have already spent more than $600,000 in direct expenditures in recent months on Central American and African migrant assistance.

"It's not an option for us to say to people newly arrived in the United States that they're not our problem and that they're welcome to sleep on the park bench until they find enough money to buy food and bus tickets for their children," Dr. Bridger said. "That's just not who San Antonio is."

CHAPTER 4

Life or Death

Hidden behind the conversations about the sheer mass of men, women and children who arrive at U.S. borders seeking refuge are the forces that drive them to the point of desperation. The decision to uproot a life and pursue better circumstances in the United States is not one taken lightly. At home, these individuals are fleeing gangs, gender-based violence and political persecution. The articles in this chapter feature stories about the violence and hardships asylum seekers are seeking refuge from.

Losing Asylum, Then His Life

BY JULIA PRESTON | JUNE 28, 2010

ONE MAN IS DEAD, shot in the mouth in El Salvador, presumably for speaking ill of a gang. Another man lives in hiding in the Salvadoran countryside, hoping his former gang will not mete out a similar punishment to him.

Both men had once fled to the United States, where they sought asylum, saying they faced mortal threats from street gangs in El Salvador. In recent years the immigration courts have seen a surge of thousands of such gang-related claims from Central Americans. They have rarely been granted.

But the cases of these two Salvadorans, Benito Zaldívar, who was killed, and Nelson Benítez Ramos, have added new credibility to those claims. They have increased the pressure on the courts and the Obama administration to clarify asylum law so foreigners facing life-threatening dangers from gangs would have a chance at refuge in this country.

Carlos Zaldívar at home in Carthage, Mo., with a picture of his son Benito, who was killed by gang members after being deported to El Salvador.

Immigration judges have rejected asylum for people running from Central American gangs on the grounds that the threats were vague and that the petitioners' lives did not appear to be truly at risk.

In Mr. Zaldívar's case, the Board of Immigration Appeals found that he had failed to show that the gang he feared, Mara-18, was specifically coming after him. Mr. Zaldívar "indicated that the gang members threatened to hurt his family if he did not join," the judges wrote, "but neither the respondent nor anyone in his family has ever been harmed."

Mr. Zaldívar was deported to El Salvador in December after his asylum petition failed. His murder just two months later was the proof he foretold that his fears of the gang were not exaggerated.

"I've done about a hundred cases of Salvadoran males who refused to join gangs," said Roy Petty, an immigration lawyer in Missouri who represented Mr. Zaldívar. "I have to tell them you are probably going to lose. The immigration system did not believe these people were really in danger."

As a boy, Mr. Zaldívar said in an immigration court statement, he was left with grandparents in La Libertad, a town on the coast of El Salvador, when his parents came in 1994 to work in the United States. Mr. Zaldívar said the Mara-18 gang had started trying to recruit him when he was not yet a teenager.

The gang was more forceful with him than with his friends, Mr. Zaldívar declared in the statement. "I think it was because the gang members knew I didn't have a big family to take care of me," he said.

Then his grandmother died. In 2003, when he was 15, Mr. Zaldívar decided he could no longer safely resist the gang, and he fled El Salvador to join his parents, legal immigrants living in Carthage, Mo.

Their temporary immigration status did not allow them to bring their son through legal channels, and Mr. Zaldívar was caught by border agents when he crossed into the United States illegally. He applied for asylum, saying that if he returned to El Salvador, the Mara-18 would exact revenge for his refusal to join.

As the case proceeded, he was permitted to rejoin his parents. "I'm going to high school in Carthage," he informed the court at one point, "and I feel safe for the first time in my life."

On Feb. 28, eight weeks after he was deported, a white van pulled alongside Mr. Zaldívar as he rode his bicycle through La Libertad. According to sworn statements in court documents, several witnesses saw a Mara-18 gunman shoot him in the face, which they understood as revenge for speaking against the gang.

Mr. Zaldívar's father, Carlos, said in an interview that entreaties from a daughter still living in El Salvador had persuaded him not to return for his son's funeral. "It left me with an empty place," Carlos Zaldívar said in anguish. "But she said the gangs could blow me away, too."

In general, legal standards for asylum in the United States are not easy to meet. Asylum seekers must show they have a "well-founded fear of persecution" because of their race, religion, nationality, political opinion or "membership in a particular social group." In 2009, a total of 9,614 foreigners were granted asylum, according to official figures. Guatemala, the Central American country with the highest number of successful petitions, had 265 grants. As the immigration debate becomes increasingly polarized, there is little interest among politicians or the public in seeing the asylum numbers increase.

While the civil wars of Central America subsided by the 1990s, the number of people seeking refuge from criminal gangs there has soared in the last decade as the maras, as they are known in Spanish, have extended their violent networks across the region. In many cities the gangs have become more powerful than the police.

"To put it bluntly, Central America is the most violent region of the world, with the exception of those regions where some countries are at war or are experiencing severe political violence," the United Nations Development Program concluded in a report in October that studied homicide rates across the globe. The bloodshed in Central American came primarily from criminal gangs.

At the same time, American immigration judges, always careful not to open the asylum door to any flood, have made it more difficult for Central Americans running from gangs. In a landmark ruling in 2008, the Board of Immigration Appeals denied a petition by three Salvadoran teenagers who fled recruitment by a gang called the MS-13, saying they had not shown that they were in more peril than Salvadorans in general.

"Gang violence and crime in El Salvador appear to be widespread, and the risk of harm is not limited to young males who have resisted recruitment," the board found.

The judges created several legal hurdles for asylum seekers fleeing gangs, requiring them to prove that they are part of a "particular social group" that is widely recognized in their home society as being under attack, something like a persecuted ethnic minority.

"The law has been kind of ripped apart," said Deborah Anker, a law professor and director of the Immigration and Refugee Clinical Program at Harvard. "Requirements have been imposed that make no sense in terms of prior jurisprudence and are impossible to interpret."

Some federal appeals courts have taken the same view. Judge Richard A. Posner of the United States Court of Appeals for the Seventh Circuit, in Chicago, has repeatedly rejected the new standards as "illogical" and "perverse."

In March, Attorney General Eric H. Holder Jr. formally declined to step in to clarify the administration's position. Senator Patrick J. Leahy, a Vermont Democrat who is chairman of the Judiciary Committee, offered a refugee bill in March that would erase the recent court decisions and return to a less complicated standard that some people escaping gangs could hope to meet. But the bill is not advancing, with Congress focused on other issues. So Mr. Benítez waits in El Salvador, after being deported last year. Recruited by the MS-18 gang when he was 14, Mr. Benítez quit after nine years when he became an evangelical Christian, and he fled to join other Christian relatives in the United States.

In December, the Seventh Circuit, in a decision written by Judge Posner, rejected the immigration court's finding that Mr. Benítez's fears did not meet the asylum test and granted his request.

But he remains in El Salvador, while his lawyer, Mr. Petty, negotiates with immigration authorities to allow him to come back to the United States.

With an indigo MS-13 tattoo etched on his forehead, he is literally a marked man. In a telephone interview last week, he said he was staying with relatives, skipping from house to house, rarely venturing outside.

"There are gangs everywhere here," Mr. Benítez said. "When you leave the gangs, even your best friend will murder you."

Inside an Immigrant Caravan: Women and Children, Fleeing Violence

BY KIRK SEMPLE | APRIL 4, 2018

MATÍAS ROMERO, MEXICO — With a sarcastic half-smile, Nikolle Contreras, 27, surveyed her fellow members of the Central American caravan, which President Trump has called dangerous and has used as a justification to send troops to the border.

More than 1,000 people, mostly women and children, waited patiently on Wednesday in the shade of trees and makeshift shelters in a rundown sports complex in this Mexican town, about 600 miles south of the border. They were tired, having slept and eaten poorly for more than a week. All were facing an uncertain future.

"Imagine that!" said Ms. Contreras, a Honduran factory worker hoping to apply for asylum in the United States. "So many problems he has to solve and he gets involved with this caravan!"

The migrants, most of them Hondurans, left the southern Mexican border city of Tapachula on March 25 and for days traveled north en masse — by foot, hitchhiking and on the tops of trains — as they fled violence and poverty in their homelands and sought a better life elsewhere.

This sort of collective migration has become something of an annual event around Easter week, and a way for advocates to draw more attention to the plight of migrants.

But this particular caravan caught the attention of Mr. Trump, apparently after he heard about it on Fox News. In a Twitter tirade that began Sunday, he conjured up hordes of dangerous migrants surging toward the border. He demanded that Mexican officials halt the group, suggesting that otherwise he would make them pay dearly in trade negotiations or aid cuts.

Mr. Trump even boasted that his threat had forced Mexico's government to halt and disperse the caravan participants. But there was no evidence of that on Wednesday.

The caravan migrants speaking with Mexican immigration officials.

Mexican migration authorities were distributing transit permits that would either give the migrants 20 days to leave the country or 30 days to formally apply for legal immigration status in Mexico.

Irineo Mujica, Mexico director of Pueblo Sin Fronteras, an advocacy group that is coordinating the caravan, called Mr. Trump's Twitter attacks and promise of a militarized border "campaign craziness."

"There are 300 kids and 400 women," he said. "Babies with bibs and milk bottles, not armaments. How much of a threat can they be?"

After making steady progress for a week through southern Mexico, the group has been camped at the sun-blasted sports complex here since Saturday, before Mr. Trump started tweeting about it, surviving on food and water donated by residents in this rural town. They have slept on the ground, or in the bleachers of a soccer stadium, or under the roofs of a few derelict structures on the property.

A stream, shrouded by bushes and trees, is the latrine for the group, which once numbered about 1,500 but now hovers around 1,100, organizers said.

The caravan population has declined as participants have received travel papers and departed, though many of the hundreds who remain hope to continue moving north in a large group, which they do for safety from criminals.

Organizers said they were seeking buses or other transportation to move the migrants to the city of Puebla, about 250 miles away, to attend planned know-your-rights workshops on immigration law in Mexico and the United States.

The group, organizers and advocates said, represented a regional humanitarian problem, not a security crisis for the United States, as Mr. Trump has suggested.

"What he's attacking is a supremely vulnerable population," said Gina Garibo, projects coordinator in Mexico for Pueblo Sin Fronteras.

In response to Mr. Trump's tweets and his plans to militarize the border, the Mexican Senate unanimously passed a nonbinding statement on Wednesday urging President Enrique Peña Nieto to suspend cooperation with the United States on immigration and security matters — "as long as President Donald Trump does not conduct himself with the civility and respect that the Mexican people deserve."

Caravan organizers also said their intent was never to storm the border, especially not with a caravan of this size. While the original plan included the possibility of escorting the caravan to the northern border of Mexico, organizers had expected the group to mostly dissolve by the time it had reached Mexico City.

But now the leaders expect to end the caravan at the capital, owing to the unwieldy size of the group, leaving migrants to decide for themselves what action to take from there.

Most caravan members interviewed here on Wednesday said their dream was to reach the United States, though some said that if they were unable to enter legally, they might seek legal status in Mexico.

Bayron Cardona Castillo, 27, said he had been traveling with his 2-year-old daughter, Glirian Dayani, from their home in Honduras and was hoping to apply for asylum in the United States. But he did not seem clear on the requirements.

"The truth is, what we're looking for is a way to live in peace, in tranquillity, with employment," he said. "In my case, all I ask is an opportunity, a chance to work and help my family."

Organizers said that once the migrants consult with volunteer lawyers in Puebla, many will conclude their cases are not strong enough to apply for legal protections in the United States and will choose to remain in Mexico.

Even without a wall and the United States military, getting into the United States is tough, Mr. Mujica said.

"You're like the waves crashing into the border and bouncing back," he said. "And you end up working in Mexico."

Mexico has increasingly become a destination for migrants from Central America. Last year, about 14,600 applied for asylum, 66 percent more than in 2016 and 11 times as many as five years ago. Many applicants in recent years have been from Honduras.

Some of the increase reflects stronger enforcement on Mexico's southern border because of a United States-backed plan to curb illegal northbound migration. Once stopped by the Mexican authorities, many detainees have come to learn they may be eligible for sanctuary in Mexico.

On Tuesday, Mr. Trump suggested that pressure he had applied on the Mexican government had stopped the caravan in Matías Romero. But organizers from Pueblo Sin Fronteras said that the caravan's momentum had simply slowed, because of its size and many vulnerable participants, especially young children and infants.

Mr. Peña Nieto's administration also appeared to push back at Mr. Trump's contention that he had coerced them.

In a joint statement, the ministries of interior and foreign relations said the caravan was halted by the participants, and not because of "any external or internal pressure."

Guillermo Baltazar Rivas, 20, from El Salvador, and his two sisters, were among the scores of migrants who were given travel permits on Wednesday. They slipped the documents into their passports for safe-keeping.

They said they did not know exactly what they would do next — head out on their own or remain with the group. Eventually, though, they hoped to apply for asylum in the United States, where close relatives lived, on the grounds that gangs murdered their brother and threatened the rest of the family with death.

With little access to news or social media among the caravan members, word of Mr. Trump's fixation on their northward journey spread via word-of-mouth.

"He says we are criminals, that we are assassins, that he isn't going to let us enter, that he's going to send the military," Mr. Rivas said. "It's very — how do I say it? — it's very selfish that he doesn't let us pass."

Ms. Contreras said she knew many caravan participants who had plans to make new lives in Mexico City, Puebla and Tijuana. But she, too, had designs on making it to the United States, as did two travel-mates. Asylum was her goal: She had been threatened with death by a drug trafficker after she had spurned his romantic advances and his efforts to recruit her into his criminal business.

The common denominator among caravan participants, Ms. Contreras said, was their agonizing decision to migrate.

"Who wants to leave their country, the comfort of their home, their families?" she asked. "It's a very difficult thing."

'Someone Is Always Trying to Kill You'

OPINION | BY SONIA NAZARIO | APRIL 5, 2019

The United States cannot erect a wall and expect women to resign themselves to being slaughtered.

CHOLOMA, HONDURAS — The murder of Sherill Yubissa Hernández Mancia explains why Central American women are fleeing north.

Ms. Hernández was a 28-year-old agent for the Agencia Técnica de Investigación Criminal, or ATIC, Honduras's F.B.I., the agency charged with investigating the killings of women. She was having an affair with Wilfredo Garcia, who was the head of the agency's office in San Pedro Sula, Honduras's second-largest city. According to people involved in the case, at some point Ms. Hernández seems to have come to believe that instead of working to take down MS-13, the nation's largest gang, her lover was married to the sister of an MS-13 leader, and was aiding the criminals.

On June 11, 2018, Ms. Hernández was found dead in her bed. Karla Beltrán, who works at the San Pedro Sula morgue, told me that in an unprecedented move, ATIC barred Forensic Medicine officials, along with the police and the prosecutor, from the crime scene. ATIC officials went alone and pronounced the death a suicide.

But when Ms. Hernández's body arrived at the morgue, Ms. Beltrán and her colleague, América Gómez, saw the obvious. Yes, a bullet had shattered her cranium. Yes, photos taken by ATIC showed her lying on her bed, holding a pistol to her temple. But there was no gun residue on her hand. Her tongue was sticking out, and there was froth around her mouth, signs of asphyxiation. There were two marks under her chin, suggesting she had been strangled by someone expert in cutting off oxygen without leaving bruises. Blood had defied gravity; instead of flowing toward the back of her head, it had poured over the front of her pink pajama top and down shorts emblazoned with the word "love." The crime scene photos showed that Ms. Hernández's cellphone had changed location three times while the scene was being "investigated," finally landing in a jar of water.

The morgue leaders announced that month that Ms. Hernández had been murdered. Soon after, they realized they were being followed and got multiple warnings that ATIC had a team of "sicarios" — assassins. In August, along with the director of Forensic Medicine, Semma Julissa Villanueva, and another colleague, they petitioned the Honduran government for protection and were assigned police officers to take them to and from work. But they still feel like sitting ducks. Dr. Villanueva has been granted a visa to travel to the United States, and Dr. Gómez and Ms. Beltrán have applied for asylum.

Mr. Garcia, who did not respond to a request for comment, has been reassigned to an administrative post pending an investigation into the death, said a spokesman for the Public Ministry in San Pedro Sula. Nearly 10 months later, no one has been charged. "We want to be emphatic and forceful that no one in ATIC belongs to a criminal group nor are they tied to the criminal acts you refer to," the spokesman said.

But Dr. Villanueva says she is afraid, adding that she is certain that Ms. Hernández "was executed and they are trying to cover it up."

"It's so rotten," said Karol Bobadilla, the head of investigations for the nonprofit group Women's Forum for Life in Honduras, when I met her at her office. How, she asked, can the leaders of an agency entrusted with investigating women's deaths be killing women themselves?

PRESIDENT TRUMP CALLS immigrants "criminals" — drug dealers and rapists intent on plundering America. But the truth, as I saw so clearly over a monthlong reporting trip in Honduras, is that migrants are fleeing a society controlled by criminals.

President Trump keeps threatening to shut off the southern border to prevent Central Americans from crossing. On March 29 he announced he was halting aid to Honduras, Guatemala and El Salvador — about $450 million a year that we now spend on strengthening civil society and chipping away at the power of gangs and drug cartels. Mick Mulvaney, the acting White House chief of staff, defended the decision by arguing that the money made little difference: "If it's working so well, why are the people still coming?"

Well, some of them are coming because they don't want to die. This is particularly true of women, who make up a greater proportion of border crossers every year.

This latest announcement comes on top of moves by the Trump administration to bar victims of domestic violence from applying for asylum. In June, Jeff Sessions, the attorney general at the time, sought to reverse a Board of Immigration Appeals decision from 2014 that added domestic violence to the list of horrors that could qualify someone for asylum. In December, a federal court ruled that he didn't have the authority to do that. But the Trump administration has persisted and is appealing the decision.

It's wrong to turn our backs on vulnerable women under any circumstances, but especially when they are coming from countries like Honduras, where the government is doing virtually nothing to protect them and is sometimes itself the predator.

Honduras is one of the world's deadliest places to be a woman — a 2015 survey ranked it in the top five countries, with El Salvador and Syria. According to official statistics, 380 Honduran women were murdered last year (slightly fewer than in recent years), in a country with roughly the population of New York City. But no one believes the government's numbers. The number of women who have "disappeared" continues to rise.

Unlike in much of the world, where most murdered women are killed by their husbands, partners or family members, half in Honduras are killed by drug cartels and gangs. And the ways they are being killed — shot in the vagina, cut to bits with their parts distributed among various public places, strangled in front of their children, skinned alive — have women running for the border.

Understanding what is going on in Honduras is crucial to understanding, and solving, what is going on at the United States border, where 268,044 migrants were stopped in the first five months of fiscal

2019, nearly twice as many as in the same period last year. A growing proportion — half — were families with children.

THE STATE OF CORTÉS is by far the worst.

Nearly one in three women murdered in Honduras in 2017 were killed here. And this city, Choloma, is probably the deadliest.

At least 262,000 people live in Choloma, which sprawls across hills and rutted roads on both sides of Honduras's main north-south freeway, a half-hour from Central America's largest port. Starting in the 1980s it became a hub for tax-free industrial parks where American, Canadian and Korean textile factories produced products for Hanes, Fruit of the Loom, Nike and Adidas. Women streamed into Choloma for a rare commodity in Honduras — jobs.

It is also a hub for the drug trade; product moves through here on its way from Colombia to the United States. Most neighborhoods are controlled by gangs or criminal organizations — 18th Street, MS-13 or La Rumba, named after a disco in Choloma's most troubled area, López Arellano. La Rumba has paid for trash pickup there, paved the main street (in part to enable faster getaways) and bribed the police. It also kills women. One night, a woman at La Rumba's disco said it was nice but another club was nicer. She was found dead the next morning, shot in the mouth.

Last year, 23 women were murdered in Choloma; some say the toll is a third more. But it's the growing cruelty with which women are killed that has most frightened women here.

In 2017, 41 percent of women and girls killed in Honduras showed signs of mutilation, disfigurement and cruelty beyond what was needed to kill them, according to the Violence Observatory at the National Autonomous University of Honduras.

Thanks to the contra war, when the United States secretly funded right-wing militia groups in Central America, there are an estimated 1.8 million guns in Honduras. And yet one in 10 female murder victims are strangled to death.

The sadism is the point. It sends a message — to other women, to rival men — that the killer is all powerful and never to be trifled with.

It's about machismo — the culture of which goes back to colonial times, when conquering Spaniards came without wives and treated the indigenous like slaves. Today, in a world ruled by gangs and narco groups, it's about engendering maximum terror in your enemies, and you do that by showing how macabre you can be in the way you torture or kill. Honduras is locked in a war of grisly one-upmanship, and women's bodies are the battlefield.

Melania Reyes, a leader of a women's aid group called the Women's Movement of the Neighborhood of López Arellano and Surroundings, has spent decades fighting against domestic violence but feels stunned by the new brutality. "They cut off everything," she said. "They strip them down, like they are a chicken."

Maria Luisa Regalado, the director of the Honduran Women's Collective, another local group, told me, "What we are seeing in Choloma has never been seen before."

MEN, OF COURSE, still make up a vast majority of murder victims, largely because they are more likely to be involved in gang conflicts or targeted for recruitment. But torture and mutilation aren't as routine an aspect of these killings as they are for women.

Women and girls are also increasingly being recruited by gangs and criminal organizations to sell drugs in Honduras. An estimated two in 10 gang members in the San Pedro Sula area are now female, something unheard-of not long ago. The gangs believe that men are more likely to buy drugs from a flirting woman and that the police are less likely to target her.

Some join willingly; since 2012 many of Choloma's factories have left for lower labor costs in Nicaragua, and people are desperate for work. There's such a glut of workers that factories advertise they won't hire anyone over 35.

Others are forced into it. Girls tell Ms. Reyes they are warned, "If you don't get into it, we will break you."

But they are broken anyway. They are killed for not meeting drug sales quotas, for not paying back money they owe to the cartel, for spurning the advances of a criminal or because they are the girlfriends of criminals who tire of them. "They see women as property," Ms. Regalado said.

Of the 115 women killed in Choloma between 2013 and Oct. 2018, half were 20 or younger, according to the Violence Observatory.

Ms. Reyes ticked off some of the girls murdered in López Arellano last year: a 14-year-old who sold lottery tickets and was abducted by a drug seller who raped her and shot her in the head five times; two 15-year-olds killed by MS-13 gangsters when they resisted an order to sell drugs; two 17-year-old cousins whose breasts and buttocks were cut off before 18th Street gangsters shot them in the head.

Katherine Nicolle Bonilla Carranza, just 14 years old, was another victim. She is buried under an almond tree in a cemetery near the apartment of her mother, Norma Adelí Carranza. Ms. Carranza sobbed as she described what happened on Dec. 19, 2017. Nicolle had been helping her mother wash clothes. She said she would be back in 10 minutes; she just wanted to chat with her friends at the corner. "Be careful," Ms. Carranza told her. She was shot five times in the head right next to the Catholic church down the street, probably by gangsters. "They wanted to take her," she told me, her face contorted by grief. "She didn't let them. So they killed her."

SOMETIMES THE DEATHS have nothing to do with the gangs. But the impunity for violent men is the same.

Heidy Hernandez's husband, Marcio Amilcar Mateo, was an alcoholic and a control freak. She says she needed his permission to even step outside their home. After he slashed her lip with a broken rum bottle, she says, her sister insisted she report the abuse to the Choloma police, but they did nothing. "Do I have to bring you a corpse for you to actually do your job?" her sister said to them.

Norma Adeli Carranza walking home in Choloma, Honduras, one of the most dangerous cities for women in the world.

According to Ms. Hernandez's account, Mr. Amilcar made $81 a week and brought home less than that. One night, the cupboards bare, she slipped out to get food at her aunt's a few blocks away. She ran into her husband, drunk. "You dog!," he said. "Begging food from strangers!" He locked his wife inside and ordered her, their 3-year-old son, and their 6- and 7-year-old daughters to their knees.

He grasped Ms. Hernandez's hair, yanked her head back and put his machete to her throat. "I'm going to kill you and your children," he said. "If you aren't with me, you won't be with anyone." He finally put the blade away with a warning: Don't go to the police.

One day she got home half an hour late from her father's house. "Who were you with?" he demanded. He pulled the machete out from under their bed and swung the blade into the back of her legs. One of their daughters, Nadia Mabel, then 8, started screaming: "Papa! Don't kill her!"

At 28, Ms. Hernandez awoke from surgery with her right leg amputated below the knee. Most of her left foot was gone. Her heart had stopped twice.

Mr. Amilcar, who had swung his machete into his wife's legs 10 times, was charged with inflicting "light lesions," carrying a sentence of 15 years. Only after their oldest daughter visited him in jail, and heard him vow, "When I get out I'm going to kill her," did a judge add attempted femicide charges and tack on 20 more years.

"My dad took off her feet," Nadia Mabel told me, nervously. "I thought he was going to kill her."

IN 2013 THE Honduran government passed a law imposing harsher sentences for femicides — gender-motivated killings in which the perpetrator was a partner, a family member, an ex, or had committed domestic violence; in which sex preceded the death; or in which the victim's body was degraded or mutilated. The label can increase a homicide sentence to 30 or 40 years. But almost no one is actually charged with femicide. The Violence Observatory says that more than 60 percent of women's murders are femicides, but the charge has been used only 33 times — during a period when 1,569 women and girls died violently.

Domestic violence laws, which didn't exist here until 1997, also remain weak. Beating someone the first time is a "fault," not a crime. A court or prosecutor's office can issue restraining orders for up to six months, but the police largely don't enforce them. Sometimes the police are so afraid to even go to a violent neighborhood that they tell the woman she has to serve her abuser the restraining order on her own. If you put a machete to your wife's throat, all the police can do is lock you up for 24 hours, and they often don't even do that on weekends, said Saida Martinez, a leader of the López Arellano women's group.

Choloma women are asking for help: Each year, about 1,400 seek out the Choloma Women's Office, a city agency that helps women with their domestic violence cases, and another 500 go directly to Choloma's courts. Some 5,000 went to San Pedro Sula's four judges last year for domestic violence issues.

But their first recourse, the police, are often less than helpful. Women tell me some of their responses: You like getting hit, don't you? Why don't you resolve it between your bedsheets? Maybe you didn't give him what he needed last night? "They mock them," Ms. Reyes said.

Elena Garcia, who is 38, asked me not to use her full name. She told me what happened to one of her friends three years ago, after she went to the police, covered in bruises. She got a restraining order against her partner and was told to deliver it herself. She disappeared that day and was later found burned, inside a bag, on the banks of the Chamelecón River.

Last Jan. 27, Norma Lilian Ávila Hernandez, a 29-year-old hair and makeup stylist, had an argument with her husband, Hugo Daniel Cruz Cabrera, 38, over her wearing makeup. According to Ms. Beltrán at the morgue, who also worked on this case, he grabbed a machete and started to cut grass around their home, looking at her menacingly. Ms. Ávila went to her local police station. Two officers were dispatched to look into her case, but they ignored their orders. When she returned to her house, her husband strangled her to death, police officials said. There is a warrant out for his arrest.

Women like her have no place to hide: There are no domestic violence shelters in Choloma or nearby San Pedro Sula. The nearest is a six-hour bus ride away.

EVEN AFTER THEY are killed, most women don't get any justice. Nine in 10 murders of women never go to court or result in a sentence. Nearly half of these murders happened in public.

I spoke to one woman, Sonia Fuentes, who survived being shot 12 times by her ex in front of a factory just as a shift was ending and workers were pouring out the gates.

By chance, two police officers happened to be turning down the street right as it happened. If they hadn't, who knows if he would ever have been charged.

Sometimes, even when prosecutors and police know exactly who killed a woman, they still don't arrest him.

Glenis Vanessa Ramirez Hercules was 17 when she met Jairo Mauricio Claro Burgos, and 26 when he killed her, her family says. He was with 18th Street, and though he beat her, she didn't trust the police to help. Mr. Claro had a cousin on the Choloma police force, and most of the officers were too afraid to even enter the neighborhood, Ms. Ramirez's aunt, Danelia Hercules, told me. When they drive here, they're always blaring their sirens or honking their horns, she said. "It's like they are announcing to the gangs: We're coming!"

Eventually Ms. Ramirez moved out and rented her own room nearby, but one night, on Oct. 30, 2016, she returned to find her husband waiting.

A local drug addict later told Ms. Hercules that Mr. Claro had strangled Ms. Ramirez in front of their three young sons. He broke her legs so that he could stuff her into a nylon bag used to sell dried corn. Two neighbors heard her cry for help, but the owner of the house said he thought it was just another fight, and all were afraid to call the authorities.

Ms. Ramirez's family noticed she was missing the next day. They believe Mr. Claro hauled the sack out Sunday night and left it, covered in grass and trash, on the side of the road a few blocks away. On Monday, the boys told their father that some were accusing him of killing their mother. Mr. Claro bolted. That's when the eldest, who was 9, dared to tell another aunt that he had been warned by his father that if he told anyone what he had witnessed, he would "do to me what he did to my mom."

When Ms. Ramirez's mother went to file a missing-person report, she said she learned that Mr. Claro's father had already gone to the police, to report that his son had confessed the murder to him.

Tuesday morning a young man collecting firewood found the 110-pound sack with Ms. Ramirez's decomposing body.

At a family wake that night, someone spotted Mr. Claro lurking nearby, and two dozen men gathered their guns and machetes to kill him, because they were sure the police would not pursue him. But he escaped.

Denis Ávila Maradiaga, head of the homicide unit at the Directorate for Police Investigations in San Pedro Sula, told me the police had put out an order to arrest Mr. Claro. But Ms. Ramirez's mother said "they did nothing to find him."

Mr. Claro has been spotted over the past two years in the nearby 18th Street strongholds of Japón and Kilómetro. Ms. Hercules shook with anger when she told me "that man is free, he will kill us all, and the authorities will do nothing." When I spoke with her this week, she said she saw him again in February. She is so frightened, she is thinking of leaving for the United States.

WOMEN'S MURDERS AREN'T investigated or prosecuted because of a toxic stew of corruption, incompetence, and a lack of both resources and interest.

A 2018 study of cases in San Pedro Sula found that more than 96 percent of women's murders go unpunished. The prosecutor's office blamed this largely on family members being afraid to testify — in a place where you can buy a hit on a person for $50 and no one believes the police can or will protect them. Of 783 killings of women in Cortés between 2013 and 2018, prosecutors here say that just 17 percent have begun a court process and an estimated 12 percent will get a verdict — statistics they trot out as an improvement.

"Government entities work with police and narcos and gangs to hide cases sometimes," said Belinda Domínguez, the coordinator of Choloma's Women's Office. She described prosecutors purposefully losing files or slow-walking cases, and corrupt cops tipping off accused criminals as soon as a complaint is filed. Prosecutors who actually did their jobs have ended up dead.

A worker at the San Pedro Sula morgue said he was offered $16,300 to change an autopsy report. Criminal organizations pay the police to look the other way, to help them get out of jail when they are arrested and to even kill for them.

Two years ago, a Choloma police officer who was also working as a sicario killed a 20-year-old woman who had refused a narco's advances. Four months later, the narcos paid to have the officer murdered, to cover their tracks, Virginia Marta Velásquez, the founder of the López Arellano women's group, told me.

In 2017, in Choloma's Cerro Verde neighborhood, a bus company was refusing to pay an extortion "tax" to the 18th Street gang. The bus stop was always guarded by the police. One night, several people told me, the police abandoned the stop and eight bus riders were gunned down. The bus company now pays the tax.

"There's a lack of interest in doing the work," said Ms. Domínguez, who has an image of the North Star on the wall of her cramped office. The morgue does an autopsy and an investigation, but four out of five times, according to employees at the San Pedro Sula morgue, their report isn't even picked up by prosecutors. Forensic Medicine has the ability to lift fingerprints from the nylon bags in which women are so often disposed, but the person who would do the test cannot recall police investigators ever requesting one. Last November, when Choloma's Women's Office held a training, funded partly by U.S.A.I.D., about how to better handle domestic violence, the police were invited but didn't come, Ms. Domínguez said.

AS A RESULT, most advances for abused women in Choloma have come through nonprofit groups whose leaders risk their lives to teach women their rights and find workarounds to government inaction.

At the offices of the Women's Movement of the Neighborhood of López Arellano and Surroundings, a steady stream of women arrive each day to ask for help with domestic violence claims or child support.

Ms. Velásquez, a regal mother of nine with short black hair, founded the group in 1992. She got into organizing after a Belgian labor rights organizer she washed clothes for suggested she attend a women's meeting in the capitol. She and a friend ended up training for a year in women's legal rights. Then they began training other women — about self-esteem, sex education and the cycle of domestic violence (he hits you, he brings roses, he hits you).

Long before there were any domestic violence laws, Ms. Velásquez and her friend would knock on the doors of abusers. "We are the authorities to stop domestic violence! If you don't cut it out, we will put you in jail!" they would shout. It often worked. Ms. Velásquez marched through the streets with a bullhorn: "We want to notify women that if your husband is hitting you, come put in a report."

Men called them sick and crazy. They said a foreigner had brainwashed them. They barred their wives from coming to meetings. And worse. In 1996, the wife of a police officer was stabbed to death in front of her 4-year-old daughter after she put in a domestic violence complaint at the group's office. In 2002, another abusive husband poured gasoline on his own house and lit a match with his wife and three children sleeping inside (they woke up and escaped in time).

Nonetheless, the women kept coming. The group helped provide 50,000 signatures to prod Honduras's congress to pass the 1997 domestic violence law. It helps women fill out forms to take to the police or courts asking for an arrest or temporary restraining order. It lobbied for funding for a walking bridge over the freeway, potable water, a kindergarten. It has provided documents to women applying for asylum in the United States. Today it has 680 members.

The group reels nervous women in by teaching them how to make things they can sell, like crocheted tablecloths. Ms. Martinez, one of the leaders, talks to women about looking at themselves naked, loving their bodies, while they crochet. Almost every surface of her house, including the toilet and the stove, is covered in doilies.

"Women were afraid to talk, to express themselves," Ms. Martinez said. "Now they talk."

She also says that domestic abuse has declined. In the early 1990s, an estimated seven in 10 men beat their wives in the area; now it's two or three of 10, she said. But the murders — they keep happening.

Zoila Lagos, one of the group's founders, now runs another women's organization in a nearby neighborhood. The night I visited her, she was trying to keep Rosa Concepción Castellano Coello alive.

Ms. Castellano's husband, a 230-pound private security guard, had been beating her for 19 years, Ms. Castellano told us. The night before, he had squeezed her throat and lifted her off the ground. He was on crack, Ms. Castellano said, which always makes him more aggressive, and he was angry that she wouldn't let his lover move in.

When the youngest of their three children, 4-year-old José Daniel, ran into the street for help, Ms. Castellano ran after him. Her husband followed, put the muzzle of his gun against her forehead and said, "I'm going to kill you, bitch," before firing four shots next to her and their son's feet. "I saw a demon in his eyes," she told us. For the first time, she felt he might finish her off.

Ms. Lagos had helped her get a restraining order, but the authorities wouldn't deliver it until the next day. Ms. Lagos urged her not to go home. "I'm afraid he will kill you," she said. "We will follow your case and help you." But Ms. Castellano doesn't trust the authorities to do anything. She wondered whether her only real chance at safety was to leave in the next caravan north.

EVERYONE IN CHOLOMA knows about the woman who was skinned alive here in June 2017.

Edelsa Muñoz Nuñez, 47, lives in an apartment near the two murder victims, Irma Quintero López, 21, and Dunia Xiomara Murillo Reyes, 34. They were tortured and killed in their home, most likely by gang members. They peeled the skin from Ms. Murillo's legs. "Like you skin a pig," Ms. Muñoz told me, shaking.

The women's body parts were found strewn around — the feet in one place, the heads in another. One torso was missing. Although four MS-13 members were arrested, the suspected ringleader of the crime remains at large.

Now Ms. Muñoz leaves her home only to buy food or go to work. On her $285-a-month salary, she can afford to take public transportation only one way, in the morning, when the mototaxi fares are half-price. At night she has to walk through a neighborhood where MS-13 and La Rumba are battling for control.

Ms. Muñoz says the police blame murder victims for going out to drink a beer, or wearing short skirts. "Why don't they do their work and actually investigate?" she demanded. "The government has to care."

"When we go out, we don't know if we will come home," said Ms. Regalado of the Honduran Women's Collective. Even as an outsider visiting Choloma for two weeks, I came to understand that deeply. One night, a teenager was shot dead on the street a block away from me. One of seven colleagues at my driver's taxi stop was murdered while I was in town.

Ms. Garcia, the woman whose friend was killed, has been gang-raped not once but twice in her 38 years. When she was 13, someone drugged her drink at a wedding and she was discovered a dozen hours later in a garbage dump, naked, unconscious, bound at the feet and hands, teeth marks and bruises all over her body. She became pregnant with her now 23-year-old daughter. She says the police never investigated anyone at the wedding to determine who kidnapped her.

Then, on July 16, 2013, she was walking home at 4 p.m. from a meeting at her children's school in Choloma when two men with black masks materialized in the drizzle. "Too bad you passed by the wrong place at the wrong time," one of them said, throwing her to the ground. They dragged her into tall grass and, with one holding a machete to her throat, took turns raping her from behind.

For six months, she washed her body with bleach to try to remove the stain of the trauma. She later heard that the same thing had happened to another woman in the same spot. Last year, she went to the police to ask about her case, but she says she was told they were closing it without charging anyone. "I am in constant fear," Ms. Garcia said. "I leave my house, but I never know if I will return. Just because you are a woman, you feel hatred. Like someone is always trying to kill you."

SO WHAT CAN BE DONE?

The United States cannot erect a wall and expect women to resign themselves to stay put in Honduras and be slaughtered.

President Trump's plan to cut off foreign aid is exactly the wrong thing to do. We could use that money to fund programs like sex education in schools, which can help break the cycle of domestic abuse, in which children who witness abuse grow up to become abusers. We could use it as a bargaining chip to force reforms. Some Honduran women's groups have suggested that the United States, as a condition for its aid, require that Honduras commit a percentage of its budget to holding abusers and killers accountable.

Government workers who don't do their jobs should be fired; those on the take should be fired. The rot starts at the top, with Honduras's president, Juan Orlando Hernández. The Organization of American States questioned the validity of his 2017 election and his brother, Tony, was arrested last year by the United States for "large-scale" drug trafficking. Instead of accepting him, the United States should push for a change in leadership.

Cutting off the border and trying to stop victims of domestic violence from applying for asylum are even greater mistakes. During World War II, the United States blocked a ship with hundreds of Jewish refugees from docking at our shores, sending many back to their deaths. After the war, the United States declared "never again" and became a leader in the modern-day refugee movement. This is at the core of who we are: We don't send people who arrive at our borders back to die. We incorporated that ideal into international treaties and our own immigration laws.

If we turn our backs now on Central American women who are running for their lives, we will be failing to meet the lowest possible bar for human rights. These women are being targeted just for being women. They are fleeing countries where the government does little to protect them and is sometimes even complicit in the killings.

Whatever the Trump administration says, the women are not criminals; they are victims. And we are perfectly capable of saving their lives. In the last fiscal year, 97,728 migrants had a credible-fear interview, the first step in the asylum process for people who fear being returned to their own country. Only a small percentage will ultimately be approved. There is no public breakdown on asylum applications by gender, but if even half of those were domestic violence cases, it would be an entirely manageable number of people for one of the richest countries in the world to take in.

For now, women keep running.

At 9 p.m. on Jan. 14, at a bus terminal in San Pedro Sula, I watched one of the latest caravans leave for the United States. It was pouring rain but they couldn't afford to wait for morning; police officers were arriving, and the migrants were afraid of being detained.

They went on foot down the dark road north, about 1,500 people, pushing carry-on luggage, strollers, a shopping cart, carrying babies in their arms.

Lilian Johann Mercado Sorian, who is 26, stopped to let her 7-year-old daughter, Andrea Johana Bardales Mercado, sleep for a bit under an empty food stand along the road. There was much pressing her and her husband to leave Honduras, she said: no stable jobs, the rising cost of food, corruption, the fact they lived in a shack.

But at the top of her list was a neighbor who once sold Ms. Mercado sandals. That neighbor was raped and murdered three weeks earlier. She had been kidnapped and cut up with a machete. The police had laughed at her husband when he reported his wife missing. They told him she had probably run off with another man.

"I am afraid," Ms. Mercado said, pressing forward into the night. "I don't want that to happen to me."

SONIA NAZARIO is the Pulitzer Prize-winning author of "Enrique's Journey: The Story of a Boy's Dangerous Odyssey to Reunite With His Mother" and a board member of Kids in Need of Defense.

VICTOR J. BLUE is a freelance photographer based in New York City. His panoramic photographs of the destroyed cities of Raqqa, Syria, and Mosul, Iraq, are currently on view at the Bronx Documentary Center.

Women Are Fleeing Death at Home. The U.S. Wants to Keep Them Out.

BY AZAM AHMED | AUG. 18, 2019

Violence against women is driving an exodus of migrants from Central America, but the Trump administration is determined to deny them asylum.

JALAPA, GUATEMALA — They climbed the terraced hillside in single file, their machetes tapping the stones along the darkened footpath.

Gehovany Ramirez, 17, led his brother and another accomplice to his ex-girlfriend's home. He struck the wooden door with his machete, sending splinters into the air.

His girlfriend, Lubia Sasvin Pérez, had left him a month earlier, fleeing his violent temper for her parents' home here in southeast Guatemala. Five months pregnant, her belly hanging from her tiny 16-year-old frame, she feared losing the child to his rage.

Lubia and her mother slipped outside and begged him to leave, she said. They could smell the sour tang of alcohol on his breath. Unmoved, he raised the blade and struck her mother in the head, killing her.

Hearing a stifled scream, her father rushed outside. Lubia recalled watching in horror as the other men set upon him, splitting his face and leaving her parents splayed on the concrete floor.

For prosecutors, judges and even defense lawyers in Guatemala, the case exemplifies the national scourge of domestic violence, motivated by a deep-seated sense of ownership over women and their place in relationships.

But instead of facing the harsher penalties meant to stop such crimes in Guatemala, Gehovany received only four years in prison, a short sentence even by the country's lenient standard for minors. More than three years later, now 21, he will be released next spring, perhaps sooner.

And far from being kept from the family he tore apart, under

Lubia Sasvin Pérez sitting on her mother's grave with her sisters Marleny, left, and Heidy. Lubia's former boyfriend, Gehovany Ramirez, murdered the sisters' mother.

Guatemalan law Gehovany has the right to visit his son upon release, according to legal officials in Guatemala.

The prospect of his return shook the family so thoroughly that Lubia's father, who survived the attack, sold their home and used the money to pay a smuggler to reach the United States. Now living outside of San Francisco, he is pinning his hopes on winning asylum to safeguard his family. They all are.

But that seems more distant than ever. Two extraordinary legal decisions by the Trump administration have struck at the core of asylum claims rooted in domestic violence or threats against families like Lubia's — not only casting doubt on their case, but almost certainly on thousands of others as well, immigration lawyers say.

"How can this be justice?" Lubia said before the family fled, sitting under the portico where her mother was killed. "All I did was leave him for beating me and he took my mother from us."

"What kind of system protects him, and not me?" she said, gathering her son in her lap.

Their case offers a glimpse into the staggering number of Central Americans fleeing violence and dysfunction — and the dogged fight the Trump administration is waging to keep them out.

Across Latin America, a murder epidemic is underway. Most years, more than 100,000 people are killed, largely young men on the periphery of broken societies, where gangs and cartels sometimes take the place of the state.

The turmoil has forced millions to flee the region and seek refuge in the United States, where they confront a system strained by record demand and a bitter fight over whether to accept them.

But violence against women, and domestic violence in particular, is a powerful and often overlooked factor in the migration crisis. Latin America and the Caribbean are home to 14 of the 25 deadliest nations in the world for women, according to available data collected by the Small Arms Survey, which tracks violence globally.

And Central America, the region where most of those seeking asylum in the United States are fleeing, is at the heart of the crisis.

Here in Guatemala, the homicide rate for women is more than three times the global average. In El Salvador, it is nearly six times. In Honduras, it is one of the highest in the world — almost 12 times the global average.

In the most violent pockets of Central America, the United Nations says, the danger is like living in a war zone.

"Despite the risk associated with migration, it is still lower than the risk of being killed at home," said Angela Me, the chief of research and trend analysis at the United Nations Office on Drugs and Crime.

The issue is so central to migration that former Attorney General Jeff Sessions, eager to advance the Trump administration's priority of closing the southern border to migrants, issued a decision last year to try to halt victims of domestic violence, among other crimes, from seeking asylum.

To win asylum in the United States, applicants must show specific grounds for their persecution back home, like their race, religion, political affiliation or membership in a particular social group. Lawyers have sometimes pushed successfully for women to qualify as a social group because of the overwhelming violence they face, citing a 2014 case in which a Guatemalan woman fleeing domestic violence was found to be eligible to apply for asylum in the United States.

But Mr. Sessions overruled that precedent, questioning whether women — in particular, women fleeing domestic violence — can be members of a social group. The decision challenged what had become common practice in asylum courts.

Then, last month, the new attorney general, William P. Barr, went further. Breaking with decades of precedent, he issued a decision making it harder for families, like Lubia's, to qualify as social groups also.

Violence against women in the region is so prevalent that 18 countries have passed laws to protect them, creating a class of homicide known as femicide, which adds tougher penalties and greater law enforcement attention to the issue.

And yet, despite that broad effort, the new laws have failed to reduce the killings of girls and women in the region, the United Nations says.

That reflects how deep the gender gap runs. For the new laws to make a difference, experts say, they must go far beyond punishment to change education, political discourse, social norms and basic family dynamics.

Though gangs and cartels in the region play a role in the violence, most women are killed by lovers, family members, husbands or partners — men angered by women acting independently, enraged by jealousy or, like Gehovany, driven by a deeply ingrained sense of control over women's lives.

"Men end up thinking they can dispose of women as they wish," said Adriana Quiñones, the United Nations Women's country representative in Guatemala.

A vast majority of female homicides in the region are never solved. In Guatemala, only about 6 percent result in convictions, researchers say. And in the rare occasions when they do, as in Lubia's case, they are not always prosecuted vigorously.

Even defense attorneys believe Gehovany should have been charged with femicide, which would have put him in prison a couple of years longer. The fact that he was not, some Guatemalan officials acknowledge, underscores the many ways in which the nation's legal system, even when set up to protect women, continues to fail them.

In the courtroom, Lubia's father, Romeo de Jesus Sasvin Dominguez, spoke up just once.

It didn't make sense, he told the judge, shaking his head. A long white scar ran over the bridge of his nose, a relic of the attack. How could the laws of Guatemala favor the man who killed his wife, who hurt his daughter?

"We had a life together," he told the judge, nearly in tears. "And he came and took that away from us just because my daughter didn't want to be in an abusive relationship."

"I just don't understand," he said.

'IT'S LIKE OUR DAILY BREAD'

Lubia's son crawled with purpose, clutching a toy truck he had just relieved of its back wheel.

The family watched in grateful distraction. Years after the murder, they still lived like prisoners, trapped between mourning and fear. A rust-colored stain blotted the floor where Lubia's mother died. The dimpled doorjamb, hacked by the machete, had not been repaired. Lubia's three younger sisters refused even to set foot in the bedroom where they hid during the attack.

Santiago Ramirez, Gehovany's brother, never went to prison, spared because of a mental illness. Neighbors often saw him walking the village streets.

Friends and family mourning during the funeral for Cristina Yulisa Godínez, 18, in Guatemala City. Ms. Godínez was killed in front of her 3-year-old son and her daughter, who was a few months old. Her son told the police that a man came in, tied her up and hanged her from the ceiling.

Soon, Gehovany would be, too. The family worried the men would come back, to finish what they started.

"There's not much we can do," said Mr. Sasvin Dominguez, sending Lubia's son on his way with the toy truck. "We don't have the law in our hands."

He had no money to move and owned nothing but the house, which the family clung to but could hardly bear. His two sons lived in the United States and had families of their own to support. He hadn't seen them in years.

"I'm raising my daughters on my own now, four of them," he said.

He woke each morning at 3 a.m., hiking into the mountains to work as a farm hand. The girls, whose high cheekbones and raven-colored hair resembled their mother's, no longer went to school. With the loss of her income from selling knickknacks on the street, they couldn't afford to pay for it.

His youngest daughter especially loved classes: the routine, the books, the chance to escape her circumscribed world. But even she had resigned herself to voluntary confinement. The stares and whispers of classmates — and the teasing of especially cruel ones — had grown unbearable. In town, some residents openly blamed Lubia for what happened. Even her own aunts did.

"There's no justice here," said Lubia, who added that she wanted to share her story with the public for that very reason. Her father did, too.

In her area, Jalapa, a region of rippled hills, rutted roads and a cowboy culture, men go around on horseback with holstered pistols, their faces shaded by wide-brimmed hats. Though relatively peaceful for Guatemala, with a lower homicide rate than most areas, it is very dangerous for women.

Insulated from Guatemala's larger cities, Jalapa is a concentrated version of the gender inequality that fuels the femicide crisis, experts say.

"It's stark," said Mynor Carrera, who served as dean of the Jalapa campus of the nation's largest university for 25 years. "The woman is treated often like a child in the home. And violence against them is accepted."

Domestic abuse is the most common crime here. Of the several dozen complaints the Jalapa authorities receive each week, about half involve violence against women.

"It's like our daily bread," said Dora Elizabeth Monson, the prosecutor for women's issues in Jalapa. "Women receive it morning, afternoon and night."

At the courthouse, Judge Eduardo Alfonso Campos Paz maintains a docket filled with such cases. The most striking part, he said, is that most men struggle to understand what they've done wrong.

The problem is not easily erased by legislation or enforcement, he said, because of a mind-set ingrained in boys early on and reinforced throughout their lives.

"When I was born, my mom or sister brought me food and drink," the judge said. "My sister cleaned up after me and washed my clothes. If I wanted water, she would get up from wherever she was and get it for me."

"We are molded to be served, and when that isn't accomplished, the violence begins," he said.

Across Guatemala, complaints of domestic violence have skyrocketed as more women come forward to report abuse. Every week, it seems, a new, gruesome case emerges in newspapers, of a woman tortured, mutilated or dehumanized. It is an echo of the systematic rape and torture women endured during the nation's 36-year civil war, which left an indelible mark on Guatemalan society.

But today, the countries with the highest rates of femicide in the region, like Guatemala, also suffer the highest homicide rates overall — often leaving the killing of women overlooked or dismissed as private domestic matters, with few national implications.

The result is more disparity. While murders in Guatemala have dropped remarkably over the last decade, there is a notable difference by gender: Homicides of men have fallen by 57 percent, while killings of women have declined more slowly, by about 39 percent, according to government data.

"The policy is to investigate violence that has more political interest," said Jorge Granados, the head of the science and technology department at Guatemala's National Institute of Forensic Sciences. "The public policy is simply not focused on the murder of women."

The femicide law required every region in the nation to install a specialized court focused on violence against women. But more than a decade later, only 13 of 22 are in operation.

"The abuse usually happens in the home, in a private context," said Evelyn Espinoza, the coordinator of the Observatory on Violence at Diálogos, a Guatemalan research group. "And the state doesn't involve itself in the home."

In Lubia's case, she fell in love with Gehovany in the fast, unstoppable way that teenagers do. By the time they moved in together, she was already pregnant.

But Gehovany's drinking, abuse and stultifying expectations quickly became clear. He wanted her home at all times, even when he was out, she said. He told her not to visit her family.

She knew Gehovany would consider her leaving a betrayal, especially being pregnant with his child. She knew society might, too. But she had to go, for the baby's sake, and was relieved to be free of him.

Until the night of Nov. 1, 2015, at around 9 p.m., when he came to reclaim her.

The New York Times tried to reach Gehovany, who fled after the killing and later turned himself in. But because he was a minor at the time of the murder, officials said, they could not arrange an interview or comment on the case.

His oldest brother, Robert Ramirez, argued that Gehovany had acted in self-defense and killed Lubia's mother accidentally.

Still, Mr. Ramirez defended his brother's decision to confront Lubia's family that night, citing a widely held view of a woman's place in Jalapa.

"He was right to go back and try to claim her," he said. "She shouldn't have left him."

He looked toward his own house, etched into a clay hillside, a thread of smoke from a small fire curling through the doorway.

"I'd never allow my wife to leave me," he said.

THE SMUGGLERS' ROAD NORTH

Mr. Sasvin Dominguez woke suddenly, startled by an idea.

He rushed to town in the dark, insects thrumming, a dense fog filling the mountains. In a single day, it was all arranged. He would sell his home and use the proceeds to flee to the United States.

The $6,500 was enough to buy passage for him and his youngest daughter, then 12. Traveling with a young child was cheaper, and often meant better treatment by American officials. At least, that's what the smuggler said.

He hoped to reach his sons in California. With luck, he could find work, support the girls back home — and get asylum for the entire family.

A week later, in October of last year, he left with his daughter. A guide crossed them into Mexico. Soon, they reached the side of a highway, where a container truck sat idling. Inside, men, women and children were packed tight, with hardly enough space to move.

A dense heat filled the space, the sun baking the metal box as bodies brushed against one another. They spent nearly three days in the container before the first stop, he said.

The days went by in a blur, a log of images snatched from the fog of exhaustion. An open hangar, grumbling with trucks. Rolling desert, dotted by cactus. Sunlight glaring off the metal siding of a safe house.

They rode in at least five container trucks, as best they can remember. Hunger chased them. Some days, they got half an apple. On others, they got rice and beans. Sometimes they got nothing.

One night, they saw a man beaten unconscious for talking after the smugglers told him to be quiet.

"I remember that moment," said his daughter, whose name is being withheld because she is still a minor. Her hands twisted at the memory. "I felt terrified," she said.

Days later, starved for food, water and fresh air, she passed out in a container crammed with more than 200 migrants, her father holding her, fanning her with whatever documents he had.

In early November, they arrived in the Mexican border town of Reynosa, and were spirited into a safe house. After weeks on the road, they were getting close.

That day, the smugglers called one of Mr. Sasvin Dominguez's sons, demanding an extra $400 to ferry the two across the river to Texas. If not, they would be tossed out of the safe house, left to the seething violence of Reynosa.

The police investigating the crime scene of a suspected killing of a woman in Guatemala City.

Mr. Sasvin Dominguez's son sent the money. Last-minute extortions have come to be expected. A day later, they boarded a raft and entered the United States.

They wandered the dense brush before they stumbled upon a border patrol truck and turned themselves in.

Mr. Sasvin Dominguez said he and his daughter spent four days in Texas, in a facility with no windows. The fluorescent glare of the overhead lights continued day and night, troubling their sleep. It was cold. The migrants called it the icebox.

When they were released in November, Mr. Sasvin Dominguez was fitted with an ankle bracelet and instructed to check in with the immigration authorities in San Francisco, where he could begin the long process of applying for asylum.

His son bought them bus tickets and met them at the station. It was the first time they had seen each other in seven years.

CALIFORNIA

On a sunny day in June, Mr. Sasvin Dominguez shuffled to a park, his daughter riding in front, hunched over the bars of a pink bicycle meant for a girl half her age. Behind him, his son and grandson tottered along, hand in hand.

They traversed a quintessential American landscape — bungalows perched on tidy green yards, wide sidewalks shaded by soaring live oaks.

He and his daughter live in the family's modest one-bedroom apartment, now bursting at the seams. The trappings of suburban life fill the backyard: toolboxes, wheelbarrows, recycling bins.

But Mr. Sasvin Dominguez remains suspended in the sadness and fear he left behind in Guatemala. His other daughters are still trapped, and there is no money to move them.

Besides, he says, the journey north, even if they could afford it, is far too dangerous for three young women and a toddler to take on their own. His only hope, he says, is asylum.

That could take years, he is told, if it happens at all. A heavy backlog of cases is gumming up the courts. He does not even have a date yet for his first hearing.

In the meantime, he lives in self-imposed austerity, scared to embrace his new life, as if doing so might belittle the danger his daughters still face.

In the park, families cooked out and blasted reggaeton. His daughter play-fought with her nephew, who never tired, no matter how many handfuls of grass she stuffed down his shirt, or how many times he retreated in tears.

She has found a better rhythm in their new life. In June, she finished sixth grade at the local school, which she loves. Her older brother keeps the graduation certificate on the small dining table.

She has dyed the tips of her hair purple, a style she's grown fond of. Her face often falls back into the wide smile of the past, when her mother enrolled her in local beauty contests.

But she grows stormy and unpredictable at times, refusing to speak. She misses her mother. Her sisters, too.

Stuck in Guatemala, Lubia and her two other sisters moved into a small apartment, where they share a single bed. A portrait of their mother hangs on the wall.

They all work now, making tortillas in town. But they go straight home after, to avoid being spotted. Not long ago, Lubia ran into Gehovany's mother.

Life for the sisters is measured in micro-improvements, pockets of air in the stifling fear. They are scarcely more than children themselves, raising children alone. Lubia's 18-year-old sister now has an infant of her own.

They sometimes visit their mother's grave, a green concrete box surrounded by paddle-shaped cactus.

"We are left here with nothing," Lubia said.

She still bears the stigma of what happened. Neighbors, men and women alike, continue to blame her for her mother's death. It doesn't surprise her anymore. Now 20, she says she understands that women almost always bear the blame for problems at home.

She worries about the world her son will grow up in, what she can teach him and what he will ultimately come to believe. One day, she will tell him about his father, she says, but not now, or anytime soon.

By then, she hopes to be in the United States, free of the poverty, violence and suffocating confines for women in Guatemala.

"Here in Guatemala," she said, "justice only exists in the law. Not in reality."

MERIDITH KOHUT in Jalapa, Guatemala, and **PAULINA VILLEGAS** in Mexico City contributed reporting.

AZAM AHMED is the bureau chief for Mexico, Central America and the Caribbean. He was previously the Afghanistan bureau chief, and has also covered the world of high finance and white-collar crime for the Business desk.

CHAPTER 5

Perspectives on Asylum

As policy makers, activists and journalists examine the impact of the Trump administration's effort to discourage people from seeking refuge in the United States, a growing debate seeks to define what a humane asylum policy would look like. The articles in this chapter examine some of the features of that debate and underscore the importance of recognizing the human costs of United States policy.

Locked Up for Seeking Asylum

OPINION | BY ELIZABETH RUBIN | APRIL 2, 2016

I RECENTLY RECEIVED a phone call from Alabama. It was Samey Honaryar, an Afghan who had worked as an interpreter with the United States military and had fled Taliban persecution hoping to find asylum here. Samey is not accused of committing any crime. Yet for nearly a year, he's been locked up in Etowah County Detention Center, among the worst and most remote of immigration detention centers, with little access to lawyers or medical attention.

"I cannot take it anymore," said Samey, who was planning a hunger strike. "I served this country. I risked my life for this country, and this is how I'm repaid."

I have reported from Afghanistan frequently since 2001, and I know that interpreters are an essential conduit into a culture easily misread by foreigners. Nearly every translator I've worked with has saved my

life. But once they choose to work for the military, their job becomes a political act, making them marked men and women for the Taliban.

At a time when Europeans and Canadians are sheltering over a million asylum seekers, many from conflicts created by United States policies, Samey's treatment demands attention. Documents and witnesses show that Samey risked his life for American soldiers. But he has been cast into immigration purgatory nonetheless, his troubles caused by a toxic mix of bureaucracy, fear, prejudice and, most poignantly, his naïve faith in American honor.

We know our asylum policy is broken. In 2014, more than 108,000 asylum applications were filed. It is not an exaggeration to say that many of these cases are life or death, yet they are handled by only 254 immigration judges, who are also juggling hundreds of thousands of non-asylum cases. Samey's case is simultaneously unique and painfully common. Yet there is a remedy.

Samey, 35, worked for the American military in Kabul from 2009 to 2012. At one point, thieves stole his car and left a note telling him to stop working with "infidels." He gave that note to the military and the C.I.A. Days later, he was run off the road. Supervisors told him to vary his route.

Then, on his way home in 2012, gunmen smashed his car window, beat him with a rifle and tried to abduct him. A crowd gathered and the gunmen fled. Samey survived but still bears a scar on his face from the assault. Shortly after, he applied for a special immigrant visa for interpreters. His request was denied.

Afraid for his life, Samey tried finding work in India, and eventually boarded a cargo ship bound for Mexico. There, he found shelter through a Mexican he had met in Kabul. After a short stay, he took a small boat across the Rio Grande. When he encountered American border guards, he asked for asylum.

On initial review, the Department of Homeland Security found his fear of persecution to be credible. Armed with evidence of his service to the military, Taliban threats and his injuries, Samey assumed that the judge, Robert Powell, would grant him asylum. So he represented himself in court.

This was his first mistake.

Mike Williams, a retired lieutenant colonel who was one of Samey's supervisors in Afghanistan, was grocery shopping in Wegmans when he got a call from the judge. Swearing an oath with his right hand, holding baby food in his left, he vouched for Samey's character and performance. He told the judge that Samey's life was in danger and that he would take responsibility for him. Samey's aunt, an American citizen who manages a fried chicken business in New York, did the same.

"I thought it would be a fairly open-and-shut case," Mr. Williams said. But when he heard the government's lawyer on the phone shouting "objection" and "leading" the witness, he began to worry. "Samey didn't know what he was doing."

The judge ordered Samey's deportation. Flabbergasted, Samey told his aunt he would rather die in Afghanistan than rot in jail awaiting appeal. His aunt begged him not to return home and hired a lawyer to appeal. Samey was shipped to a detention center in Alabama.

Court documents suggest Samey was right to be stunned by Judge Powell's findings. "Common sense," the judge wrote in his decision, suggested that real Taliban "would have assassinated him on the spot or taken him by force." He also mused that the threatening note could have been left by car thieves.

An immigration lawyer I consulted who represents detainces at Etowah called the judge's assertions about the Taliban "rank speculation" and said she was dumbfounded that he rejected the note Samey gave to the C.I.A.

"Nobody has evidence that good for asylum," she said. "Under this judge's standard no one with these types of cases could prove the nexus requirement of asylum."

But the most extraordinary passage of Judge Powell's decision is his rejection of Samey's claim of persecution:

"Respondent must show that the Government was, or is, unable to control the Taliban. Although the Taliban is conducting a tenacious insurgency and terrorist campaign, country reports show that Afghan security forces are effective in controlling the Taliban in many parts of Afghanistan."

The year 2015 was one of the bloodiest years in Afghanistan since 2001. As of today, the Taliban have infiltrated many provinces, including the capital. The Afghan Army is taking so many casualties that it can no longer recruit enough replacement troops. The government has all but ceded sections of the country to the insurgents.

Perhaps Judge Powell was doing his best under impossible conditions. Experts have urged the government to hire more judges and staff. The president of the National Association of Immigration Judges, Judge Dana Leigh Marks, said that judges are overwhelmed by the volume of cases. It's as if death penalty cases are being handled in traffic court.

"How do you keep your heart open and remain compassionate?" she said. "I have over 3,000 pending cases. Federal District Court judges have 440, and two to three full-time lawyers. If we are lucky we have half a judicial law clerk."

The day after Samey went on hunger strike, I emailed the Board of Immigration Appeals asking why his case had not been decided after eight months. The following day, the board announced that it would send his case back to Texas for a retrial. Would that have happened without a letter from a journalist? And what does it say about the system if a case as strong as Samey's fails?

For one thing, it says that the system is stacked against the asylum seeker. The immigration judge works for the Department of Justice, and the government's attorney works for the Department of Homeland Security. Meanwhile, the asylum seeker generally has no right to a public defender. Legal representation is crucial: One study found that mothers with children without a lawyer were granted asylum 2 percent of the time while those with a lawyer won 32 percent of the time.

In New York City, an immigration public defender system developed in conjunction with Cardozo Law School and funded by the New York City Council attempts to address this problem by providing legal assistance to detainees through the Bronx Defenders, Brooklyn Defender Services and the Legal Aid Society. Immigrant Justice Corps, a nonprofit legal aid group, is sending fellows to Texas to assist asylum seekers.

Today, Samey is back in detention in Port Isabel, Tex., awaiting retrial and unable to afford a lawyer. International law holds that asylum seekers should be detained only in unusual circumstances. Yet our detention centers are filling up with people like Samey.

"People say to me: 'I came to your door. I did what I was supposed to do. And you put me in prison. I thought the United States was a human-rights country. You are not,' " said Grace Meng, a senior researcher at Human Rights Watch.

If the United States believes in the principles of asylum, we need to give traumatized people — particularly those persecuted for protecting Americans — a chance to be heard with an expert on their side.

ELIZABETH RUBIN has reported extensively from Afghanistan and the Middle East.

We Need to Offer More Than Asylum

OPINION | BY ROBERTO SURO | JULY 14, 2018

MONEY, LOVE AND FEAR. Three good reasons to find a new country. In the United States immigration system, to find work, to be with family, to flee danger are mutually exclusive categories.

But all three are intertwined for the Central Americans now on our border, and these migrants are crashing the system. These people have been forced from their homes by bloodshed and lost livelihoods. They seek shelter with relatives.

Where would you go?

As presidents, Barack Obama and Donald Trump don't have much in common, but they both failed to manage the migration out of the "Northern Triangle" of Central America — Guatemala, Honduras and El Salvador. Both tried to achieve deterrence through enforcement. Both faced political blowback. Both made awkward course corrections, like the Trump administration's shift last week from zero-tolerance lock 'em up to release them with ankle bracelets. Mr. Obama's efforts had little lasting impact. Mr. Trump has taken deterrence to a previously unimaginable extreme, committing extortion with child hostages to dissuade asylum seekers.

Whether the goal is to provide humanitarian protection to the deserving or to keep out the unwanted, current policies are failing. Some 50,000 unaccompanied children from the Northern Triangle and nearly 40,000 adults with children were apprehended at the border during the 2014 surge. The numbers jumped again in 2015 and 2016, and here we are today, with no end in sight.

A lasting solution must recognize that these surges are not isolated events but rather desperate developments in a decades-long migration. People who make up nearly 10 percent of the populations of those countries are already living here. It is a migration with momentum, and it comes from close by. They can walk to our border.

Enforcement alone won't stop them, certainly not enforcement consistent with our laws. So the root causes must be addressed. In the meantime, the families will keep coming. As we're seeing yet again, our asylum system is dysfunctional. What we need is a new visa program designed for the number and characteristics of the people arriving at the American border.

Getting to a solution starts with acknowledging that the absolute best outcome for them — and for us — is for them not to be forced out of their homes in the first place.

Mr. Trump's 2019 budget seeks $26 billion for immigration enforcement and detention, plus $18 billion more for the border wall. That's almost the combined gross domestic product of El Salvador and Honduras ($48 billion). A fraction of the enforcement budget well spent on economic development would reduce migration pressure. It would be a better use of taxpayer dollars than trying to intercept people in flight at a militarized border and then criminalizing them.

Aside from the utility, it is the right thing to do. American interventions, political, military and economic, helped create the conditions prompting many migrations, including this one.

Solving this problem, so close to home, is in our national interest. But even if we made an all-out effort to address the ills forcing people to emigrate from the Northern Triangle, we would need to manage the flow for years to come. We do not have the means to do that now.

The first problem is that our criteria for humanitarian admissions were conceived more than 60 years ago and no longer match reality. The original 1951 United Nations convention on refugees envisioned people fleeing "a well-founded fear" of persecution. Easily recognized characteristics like religion, race or political beliefs determined eligibility, and governments were the usual culprits. The Cold War drew stark distinctions between the free and the oppressed.

Today, criminal gangs, armed insurgents and other nonstate actors routinely wreak havoc. Whether their victims get protection depends on individual governments and the policies of the moment.

With the stroke of a pen on June 11, Attorney General Jeff Sessions reversed Obama-era precedents that had extended protection to some victims of domestic abuse and criminal violence. "The prototypical refugee flees her home country because the government has persecuted her," Mr. Sessions wrote in a decision now being contested by immigrant and human rights advocates.

Regardless of whether it is legally appropriate, that antique view does not describe contemporary realities. Often, the problem is not an oppressive government at all. Instead, weak governments, some of them democracies, provoke flight by failing to protect their citizens from disasters both natural and man-made.

Uncontrolled violence combines with environmental degradation and economic collapse to produce what Alexander Betts, a professor at Oxford, has termed "survival migration." The term, he writes, describes "people who have left their country of origin because of an existential threat for which they have no domestic remedy."

The 1951 standards can be stretched to cover those who flee under such conditions. However, Mr. Sessions and European restrictionists deploy the letter of the law, no matter how outdated, as grounds for rejection. And at the same time, they abrogate the migrants' right, enshrined in those same international agreements, to seek protection even if it means violating immigration rules.

Migrants from Honduras, Guatemala and El Salvador who apply for asylum face a brutally adversarial process that is stacked against them. Denial rates have been running about 80 percent in recent years, according to the TRAC data repository at Syracuse University. Applicants from countries like China, Eritrea and Ethiopia see most of their cases approved. That is a matter of policy, not of law.

The United States has repeatedly taken one-off approaches to humanitarian migrations, raising and lowering the bar according to perceived national interests. Special deals have been cut for Hungarians, Cubans, Soviet Jews, Nicaraguans and many others. Now it is time for a unique solution for the Northern Triangle.

Managing this migration effectively and humanely requires a legislative solution outside the asylum system, a solution that establishes a legal process based on the specific circumstances of this migration. Chief among those circumstances are its size and durability.

More than three million people from these countries now live here, and most have been here for more than 10 years, according to Pew calculations. The annual flow of people from the Northern Triangle, about 115,000 new arrivals in 2014, has been increasing at more than twice the rate of immigration overall, Pew says.

When conditions become life-threatening, migration is salvation at the ready. Although the journey is perilous and expensive, the channels between there and here are accessible and efficient. How else do thousands of children travel 1,500 miles unaccompanied?

Creating an effective legal option for the migrants that the Obama and Trump administrations failed to deter will require adjustments to the immigration system, but no more than special cases in the past did. Instead of treating the Northern Triangle migrants as individual asylum seekers, a new category of admissions would take their mixed motives into account — fear, love and money all bundled together. More migrants will be admitted, but not likely many more than the 300,000-plus now relegated to an ever-growing backlog of asylum cases.

President Trump shows little interest in effective policies, preferring to exploit the crisis for political ends. That means the crisis requires a political response. Condemning the administration's excesses is necessary but not sufficient. Trying to improve on the Obama version of deterrence is futile. Congressional Democrats need to propose a long-term legislative solution, making a commitment to address root causes and creating an orderly legal channel for the migration in the meantime. Then, Democrats need to campaign on it, showing the country and the world that Americans can be both humane and practical in welcoming displaced people. So far, they have not.

ROBERTO SURO is a professor of journalism and public policy at the University of Southern California. Mr. Suro was the founding director of the Pew Hispanic Center.

Seeking Refuge, Legally, and Finding Prison

OPINION | BY FRANCISCO CANTÚ | MAY 31, 2019

FOR MORE THAN seven months, Ysabel has been incarcerated without bond at an immigrant detention center in southern Arizona, part of a vast network of for-profit internment facilities administered by private companies under contract with the Department of Homeland Security.

I visit Ysabel (who has asked not to be identified by her real name for her protection) every two weeks as a volunteer with the Kino Border Initiative, one of a handful of migrant advocacy groups running desperately needed visitation programs in Arizona, including Mariposas Sin Fronteras and Transcend. As volunteers, our primary role is to provide moral support; facilitate communication with family members and legal service providers; and serve as a sounding board for frustration, confusion and, often, raw despair.

Ysabel and the other asylum seekers we visit often ask for simple forms of support, such as small deposits into their commissary accounts to let them call relatives or purchase overpriced goods like dry ramen, tampons, shampoo or headphones for watching telenovelas. They often ask us to send them books in Spanish — one of the few things that they are permitted to receive through the mail without clearance from a property officer. Large-print Bibles are the most popular, along with books of song and prayer, bilingual dictionaries and English course books, romance novels, and other books that provide ways to pass the time — word puzzle collections, coloring books, books for learning how to draw and instruction manuals for making origami figurines.

Ysabel arrived at the United States border last October after leaving her home and two children in eastern Venezuela. The region she fled was plagued by disorder long before the more widely reported upheavals of recent months, suffering frequent power outages, widespread violence and unrest, and severe shortages of food, water and medication. In the years leading up to her flight from the country, Ysabel told me that she had been kidnapped, robbed at gunpoint multiple times and shot at during an attempted carjacking.

Like millions of her compatriots, Ysabel became disillusioned after her government failed to provide even the most basic security and public services. She joined a local opposition movement, and after participating in several antigovernment demonstrations, she was marked as an enemy of the governing regime. After her house was raided by Venezuelan intelligence forces, she decided to leave for good.

To get to the United States, Ysabel went to Caracas before embarking on nearly three weeks of circuitous travel via airplane, car, bus and taxi. She journeyed through Panama City, Bogotá, Cancún, Mexico City and Mexicali, before finally arriving in San Luis Rio Colorado, a Mexican border town adjacent to Yuma, Ariz., where she presented herself to be considered for asylum at the designated port of entry.

Ysabel, it should be noted, has now been detained for more than half a year despite following American immigration and asylum laws to the letter. When interviewed by officials from the Department of Homeland Security, she was quickly found to have a legitimate fear of returning to Venezuela. Nevertheless, like tens of thousands of asylum seekers like her, she has been made to endure the suffocating precarity of our criminal justice system despite never having committed, nor ever being accused of, a crime.

Instead of appearing in criminal court, those who seek asylum in the United States undergo civil proceedings. Public defenders are not provided in civil court, so most migrants and asylum seekers receive no legal counsel as they fight their immigration cases, instead relying entirely on pro-bono legal services like The Florence Project, Arizona's only nonprofit dedicated to representing migrants. According to a 2016 report by the American Immigration Council, only 14 percent of immigrant detainees are represented by an attorney — a number that has likely fallen with recent increases in asylum seekers arriving at the border. The overwhelming majority of those without lawyers — almost 91 percent — have their cases rejected.

America's immigration system takes the myth of due process and turns it on its head. Instead of a presumption of innocence, migrants face the assumption of inadmissibility. They are tasked with demonstrating that they face a certifiable risk to their lives, though in most of their home countries there are few tangible ways to document their plight. Asylum seekers are thus saddled with a confounding burden of proof in an entirely unfamiliar legal system.

Our detention and deportation system is further obscured by a Kafkaesque, multi-agency bureaucracy that must be navigated in a language foreign to most of those ensnared in it. Even along the border with Mexico, prison guards and judges often do not speak or understand Spanish, distancing them even further from the population over whom they wield staggering control. This, in turn, exacerbates the vulnerability of detainees and their families, who are commonly preyed upon by lawyers, bail bondsmen and a microeconomy of individuals offering dubious document preparation, translation support and myriad other "services."

In Arizona, the immigration judges who decide cases inside detention facilities are often notorious for their hard-line approach. For instance, from 2013 to 2018, one southern Arizona judge, John W. Davis, denied 96.9 percent of his cases, granting only nine asylum claims out of the 291 that came before him (the nationwide denial rate during this same period was dramatically lower, at 57.6 percent). In one two-year stretch, Judge Davis ordered the deportation of every single asylum seeker who entered his courtroom.

Despite all the odds stacked against her, Ysabel was granted asylum by a federal immigration judge in February, winning her case even without a lawyer. When I visited her a few days after the decision, she was visibly changed, carrying herself with a lightness I have rarely seen inside the walls of the detention center. After half a year suffering the oppression of uncertainty, a path had finally been laid out before her. Any day now, she told me, she would be released, the exit door into America finally opened.

Days and weeks passed, however, and still the door remained inexplicably shut. Week after week, I arrived at the detention center expecting Ysabel's name to have disappeared from our list, only to find her sitting again in the visitation room among the other women seeking refuge — mothers, grandmothers, sisters, daughters. Each time we spoke, her freedom seemed to be slipping further away. The government had asked that her release be delayed while officials prepared an appeal. The deadline to file came and went without Ysabel receiving any updates regarding her case. Finally, she heard that the government had indeed filed its appeal, but she was given no follow-up court date — the one piece of information that allows detained asylum seekers to build a potential timeline for their near future, the single point around which some glimmer of hope might coalesce.

Ysabel's case, I later determined after an hour of being referred from one phone line to another, had been transferred to the Board of Immigration Appeals — America's highest administrative body for interpreting and applying immigration law. When I finally got ahold of someone from the office to inquire whether a court date had been set for Ysabel's case, I was told that there was none. Instead of holding hearings, the court decides most cases behind closed doors, usually based solely on "paper review." When I asked if the office could estimate how long it might take for a decision to be reached, I was told bluntly "there's no timeline for the board."

The power the government wields over Ysabel's fate is difficult to fully grasp. The purgatory she and other asylum seekers are made to endure often lasts for months or even years. All across the country, migrants like her are being shut off from public view in hundreds of facilities that are largely unaccountable to the outside world. Few other countries are engaged in imprisoning noncriminals at such a scale: According to the Geneva-based Global Detention Project, the American immigration detention system is the largest in the world, and one of the few that locks up migrants in criminal-style prisons.

An internal report conducted by U.S. Immigration and Customs Enforcement (ICE) in 2009 plainly states that the agency's detention model "relies primarily on correctional incarceration standards designed for pretrial felons," standards that, ICE admits, "impose more restrictions and carry more costs than are necessary." But these costs represent immense profits for the private detention industry: In fiscal year 2016, roughly two-thirds of all detained migrants (more than 260,000 people) were held in for-profit facilities, generating more than $4 billion in revenue.

Prolonged detention magnifies the most dehumanizing elements of the migrant experience — the commodification of bodies that occurs as migrants are trafficked, the dangers they endure along our militarized border and the criminalization thrust upon them from the moment they cross it. All of that is concentrated within the walls of the detention center. The women I meet feel this keenly. "I hope I can soon leave these four walls," they tell me, because within them, "it's like we are animals."

The acute power of this dehumanization is also meant to serve as a tool of deterrence. Deterrence, after all, has become the underlying philosophy of border enforcement — the ever-growing danger and expense of crossing our Southwestern deserts, the horrifying prospect of parents being separated from their children, the destabilizing uncertainty of being imprisoned with no end in sight. All of it is meant to discourage, dissuade and ultimately break the spirit of the would-be migrant.

One of the women I visit regularly, a 57-year-old grandmother from Guatemala, recently admitted to me that she was considering dropping her asylum claim in order to be deported as soon as possible. The power she felt crushing her after more than half a year of detention was becoming even more unendurable than the overwhelming fear that led her to flee her home in the first place. "No puedo aguantar mas," she told me — "I can't take it any longer."

This, I wanted to tell her, was the system working as it was designed. Instead, I told her not to lose faith, not to give up, wondering all the while if the refuge she sought here might be withheld from her forever.

FRANCISCO CANTÚ is a former Border Patrol Agent and the author of "The Line Becomes a River: Dispatches From the Border."

Children Shouldn't Be Dying at the Border. Here's How You Can Help.

EDITORIAL | BY THE NEW YORK TIMES | JUNE 24, 2019

Speak up. Donate. Educate yourself. Vote.

This editorial has been updated to reflect news developments.

THE UNITED STATES needs an immigration policy that combines border security, justice and humanity. No one with a conscience can look at the photo of an asylum seeker and his 23-month-old daughter lying dead on the bank of the Rio Grande and accept the status quo.

That single tragedy, reminiscent of the photo of a drowned Syrian boy washed up on a Turkish beach in 2015, has the power to clarify a vast, long-running problem that has already claimed many lives. What it should also do is prompt urgent action from the country's elected representatives to compromise over their many differences and resolve a stalemate that is no longer tolerable.

President Trump has made agreeing on an approach to immigration in the United States more difficult. He has done so by systematically creating a false narrative of immigrants as job-stealing criminals, by insisting that there is a crisis of illegal immigration where there is none and, most maliciously, by dreaming up schemes to torment these people in the perverse notion that this will deter others from trying to reach the United States.

The most appalling of these has been the separation of children from their parents and detaining them in conditions no child anywhere should suffer, and certainly not children in the care of the American government. At a recent hearing before a federal appeals court in San Francisco, judges were stunned by the administration's arguments that children sleeping on concrete floors in frigid, overcrowded cells, without soap or toothbrushes, were being kept in "safe and sanitary" facilities, as required by law. "You're really going to stand up and tell us that being able to sleep isn't a question of safe and sanitary conditions?" asked one judge. (John Sanders, acting commissioner of Customs and Border Protection, the agency responsible for temporarily housing the migrant children, announced Tuesday that he would be leaving his post at the end of next week.)

Mr. Trump's latest display of cruel bluster was the announcement, and then the delay, of nationwide raids to deport undocumented families. In fact, deporting immigrants who have exhausted their legal claims is not uncommon — President Barack Obama, remember, was often referred to by immigration groups as "deporter in chief" — and the targets of these raids are not random. But Mr. Trump sought to use the operation to strut before his base and extract concessions from Democrats, and spread panic through immigrant communities. His announcement delayed action by Congress and made the operation that much more difficult by warning those targeted for deportation. Then he tweeted that he was delaying the raids for two weeks.

The stalemate on immigration is a choice that Americans do not have to accept. You can help end it. Here's how:

Call Congress, your mayor and local representatives. Contact your members of Congress and tell them that you want impending raids by Immigration and Customs Enforcement to be called off and detention conditions improved. The legal defense nonprofit Raices has provided a template and an online form that you can use to email your congressional representatives. You can also reach out to your local officials to ask that they initiate plans to help immigrant communities that are affected by the raids. The official government website (https://www.usa.gov/local-governments) provides links to finding your city, county and town officials.

Report and document raids and arrests. The National Immigration Law Center has suggested reporting raids to local hotlines, such as United We Dream's MigraWatch. Raices has urged that people verify any social media posts saying ICE has been spotted before sharing or retweeting them because false alarms could spread fear in immigrant communities.

Donate to humanitarian efforts. Many immigrants are not informed of their legal and civil rights as they pursue asylum or face deportation. Several nonprofits are providing free legal representation and other services for immigrants and the families of those detained. United We Dream, the American Civil Liberties Union, Mijente, Immigrant Families Together, Save the Children and the Immigrant Justice Corps are coordinating advocacy and services at a national level. Local organizations providing legal aid include the New Sanctuary Coalition in New York, Las Americas in El Paso and Raices in Texas, Americans for Immigrant Justice in Florida and the Denver Immigrant Legal Services Fund in Colorado.

Pilar Weiss, project director of the National Bail Fund Network, says one of the most effective ways to reunite immigrants separated from their families is to assist with paying their bail, which can cost anywhere from $1,500 to $80,500. You can find and donate to a bail fund in your city through the National Bail Fund Network.

Inform yourself and your community. The A.C.L.U., which joined forces with Brooklyn Defender Services, has shared a "Know Your Rights" page for encounters with ICE. It has also provided a video to help understand your rights and what to do if ICE officials come to your home.

Hold political candidates accountable. While the presidential primaries are at least seven months away, you can prepare to cast your ballot for a more humane border policy by following what each candidate has shared about his or her plans for immigration reform.

Speak up. Protest marches and other civic actions to end detention camps and squalid conditions for children and families are expected across the country in the coming weeks. You can also take part in Lights for Liberty, a nationwide vigil on July 12. Locations for the vigil include:

• El Paso, where migrants are being housed "partially outdoors" near a bridge with no running water for months at a time;

• Homestead, Fla., where a migrant children's detention facility has been charged with rampant abuse and neglect;

• San Diego, near the point-of-entry border crossing from Tijuana, Mexico;

• New York City, where deportation rates increased by 150 percent between 2016 and 2018; and

• Washington, D.C., in front of the Capitol building, to demand action from Congress.

Asylum Officers' Union Says Trump Migration Policy 'Abandons' American Tradition

BY MIHIR ZAVERI | JUNE 26, 2019

A UNION REPRESENTING federal asylum officers said in a court filing Wednesday that the Trump administration's policy forcing migrants to wait in Mexico while their asylum cases are decided risks violating international treaty obligations and "abandons our tradition of providing a safe haven to the persecuted."

The union, which represents 2,500 Department of Homeland Security employees, including the asylum officers, said in its filing that the policy, the Migration Protection Protocols, puts migrants in danger because they could face persecution while being forced to wait in Mexico, undermining the purpose of asylum.

Citing a State Department report, the union said that "impunity for human rights abuses remained a problem" in Mexico. Migrants are at particular risk of being sexually assaulted, it said, and ethnic minorities could face "persecution similar to the persecution they face in their home countries."

"Asylum officers are duty bound to protect vulnerable asylum seekers from persecution," the union said. "They should not be forced to honor departmental directives that are fundamentally contrary to the moral fabric of our nation and our international and domestic legal obligations."

Muhammad Faridi, a lawyer representing the union, Local 1924 of the American Federation of Government Employees, said in an interview that the court filing was significant given the officers' role in returning migrants to Mexico.

"These are people working in the background. These are not people opining or expressing their opinions on public policy or litigation matters," Mr. Faridi said. "It takes something as egregious as the M.P.P., something that is so fundamentally contrary to the moral fabric of our country and international treaty obligations, it's something like that that brings people to the litigation arena."

The filing was a striking rebuke of a central part of President Trump's immigration strategy, coming from federal employees intimately involved in deciding whether those seeking refuge in the United States should be allowed to stay. As part of a deal with Mexico that Mr. Trump said stopped him from raising tariffs, Mexico committed to work to expand the program, according to the administration.

The White House did not immediately answer requests seeking comment on the brief on Wednesday night. The Department of Justice declined to comment.

The administration announced the policy in December, arguing that it would help stop people from using the asylum process to enter the country and remain illegally.

Mr. Trump had long been angered by policies that temporarily allowed asylum seekers in the United States while they waited for their court hearings. Asylum seekers have also shown up in increasing numbers in the past few months as more Central American migrants traveling through Mexico have arrived at the United States' border.

More than 11,000 migrants have been returned to wait in Mexico under the policy, according to senior homeland security officials.

The Trump administration policy was criticized for putting the migrants at risk, and legal advocates for migrants pointed to a spike in violence and overburdened shelters in Mexican border towns. Several Democratic presidential candidates at Wednesday's debate said the policy was one of the worst abuses of the Trump administration.

The administration has said the policy also aims to ease overcrowded border facilities strained by the increase in migrants.

In a lawsuit filed in February in federal court in San Francisco, the American Civil Liberties Union and other groups said the policy violated immigration law.

A federal district judge, Richard Seeborg, blocked the policy in April, saying that the president did not have the power to enforce it and that it violated immigration laws. Judge Seeborg said the program lacked safeguards to ensure that migrants were not returned to a place where they faced risks.

The Trump administration appealed the case to the Ninth Circuit, which is based in San Francisco, and on April 12 the court allowed the policy to be enforced while the case is pending.

The union's filing Wednesday was a "friend of the court" brief in the case. In the filing, the union traced the United States' long history of embracing migrants, including Irish immigrants fleeing famine and disease in the mid-1800s and refugees of Communist-dominated countries a century later. The union said the Trump administration's policy should be blocked.

"Now, perhaps more than ever, America needs to continue its long-standing tradition of offering protection, freedom, and opportunity to the vulnerable and persecuted," the union said.

ZOLAN KANNO-YOUNGS contributed reporting.

Trump Is Trying to Kill the Program That Saved My Life

OPINION | BY MARIUS KOTHOR | OCT. 2, 2019

Reducing the number of people allowed to resettle in America will leave thousands trapped in horrendous situations.

THE SEA-WASHED, sunset gates of the United States are being closed to the huddled masses yearning to breathe free. President Trump and his administration have slashed the Refugee Resettlement Program, which allows people fleeing war, persecution and famine to legally move to the United States.

On Thursday, the administration announced that it would accept only 18,000 refugees during the next 12 months, a stark reduction from the already low current limit of 30,000. By comparison, roughly 85,000 refugees were resettled in 2016 under the Obama administration.

The administration has justified the move by claiming the need to focus its energy on the humanitarian and security crisis along the southern border and on the backlogged immigration cases in American courts. Earlier, a Trump administration official had claimed that refugees pose "enormous security challenges" to the country. But coming to the United States as a refugee is the most difficult way to enter this country, because refugees go through a very thorough vetting process.

I know this because it took my family seven years to be approved for refugee resettlement in the United States after we had to flee political strife in the West African country of Togo. During those seven long years, I lost two brothers to disease and malnutrition. I became ill and bedridden but fought to survive because I did not want my mother to cry again the way she had cried when my brothers died.

Our problems began in 1993 when Eyadema Gnassingbé, then the president of Togo, started a campaign of political violence and intimidation to crush popular demands for democratic elections and free speech.

My father, a soldier in the Togolese army, was forced to watch the execution of 14 of his colleagues in Lomé, the capital. Mr. Gnassingbé ordered the executions to punish soldiers he believed supported democratic reforms and to terrorize others into complete obedience. My father feared that he would eventually be asked to prove his loyalty by participating in these murders. He fled to Benin, bordering Togo in the east.

For weeks, my mother was unable to locate my father. She took my brothers and me across Togo's western border to her maternal homeland in Ghana. Several months later, we found out that my father had made it to Benin. We traveled back through Togo to join him.

We applied for political asylum in a refugee camp the United Nations set up in Benin to assist the thousands fleeing Togo. We lived in various refugee camps, battling disease, malnutrition and the constant fear of being found out. We mostly ate a meal of water and corn flour with a soup made of palm oil and salt. We could not afford seasonings or vegetables.

Apart from the constant food insecurity, we had to hide our real identities; we could never reveal that our father had been a soldier in the Togolese military. There were men looking for him. Every time we saw strangers in our neighborhood, we panicked because we feared they had come for our father.

After six years, in 1999, we were selected by the State Department to interview in Cotonou, Benin's largest city, for resettlement. We could not afford the fare to get there. My parents sold all our belongings to get the money for the journey. Once there, we relocated to another refugee camp and went through several rounds of interviews with American and United Nations agencies, repeatedly recounting why we fled Togo and why we could not go back.

After the State Department determined that my parents were telling the truth and our situation was dire, we went through background and health checks before it finally approved us for resettlement. We were lucky: Only 1 percent of the millions of refugees around the world will ever receive a lifeline like the one we received.

On a bitter cold February morning in 2000, we arrived in upstate New York. The new beginning was difficult. Learning a new language and adjusting to American culture and customs proved demanding. With limited English language skills, my parents struggled to find work that could support our family.

I was 9. I had never been to school, could neither read nor write and spoke no English. An amazing group of committed teachers helped. It took me three years to learn to read and write.

I went to a great public school with teachers and guidance counselors who encouraged my curiosity and taught me that it was fine to ask for things like extended time on exams and after-school tutoring.

Now I am a graduate student at Yale, working on a Ph.D. in history, working toward being a historian, motivated by my desire to understand how a country like Togo came to be such a politically unstable place.

The refugee resettlement program is why I am alive today and able to dream of becoming a historian. Drastically reducing the number of refugees allowed to resettle in America will leave thousands of vulnerable people trapped in horrendous situations like what my family endured.

There are few places in the world where stories like mine are possible. We are alive and thriving because of a remarkable program that helped my family escape political persecution and allowed us to build a new life here — and showed us the best of America, a country we are proud to call home.

MARIUS KOTHOR is a Ph.D. student in history at Yale.

Asylum Protesters Close Bridge on Texas-Mexico Border

BY MIRIAM JORDAN | OCT. 10, 2019

AMID GROWING TENSION over deteriorating conditions at the border, hundreds of migrants who had been blocked from entering the United States shut down an international bridge in South Texas on Thursday, disrupting a normally busy connection between the United States and Mexico.

Between 250 and 300 migrants marched overnight to a point midway across the Gateway International Bridge between Matamoros, Mexico, and Brownsville, Texas, sitting in the vehicle lanes and blocking traffic in both directions for about 15 hours.

Customs and Border Protection halted traffic across the Gateway bridge and another international crossing nearby at about 1:30 a.m., an agency spokesman said, in response to protesters who were not carrying documents for legal entry into the United States.

Traffic resumed before dawn at the second crossing, but the Gateway bridge remained closed in both directions until late afternoon on Thursday, the spokesman said, with all vehicle traffic diverted to other ports of entry.

The episode unfolded amid escalating tension over the Trump administration's increasingly rigid policies aimed at restricting the entry of migrants into the United States. The Gateway bridge is adjacent to a teeming encampment where about 1,000 migrants, mainly from Central America, have been living in squalid conditions while they await immigration court hearings in the United States.

In recent interviews, families have described children falling ill, families plagued by thugs and a growing sense of despair as United States authorities continue to send people back from the border.

"They are absolutely desperate, with no international presence in the camp to organize anything such as food delivery or medical care," said Jodi Goodwin, an immigration attorney who holds regular workshops to help migrants fill out asylum applications and learn about the legal process.

The migrant protest, which included children, occurred as the Trump administration has moved to contain a record-breaking surge in migrant families, with the biggest numbers crossing into South Texas.

Border authorities took nearly one million people into custody in the fiscal year that ended Sept. 30, the highest number since 2007. But the new restrictive measures have brought about a sharp decline, with Customs and Border Protection reporting this week that about 52,000 migrants were taken into custody in September, an 18 percent decrease from August.

For decades, those who could reasonably argue they were fleeing persecution in their homelands could enter the United States and wait for their hearings in court. Often they stayed with relatives in the interior of the country.

But under a Trump administration program introduced in January, many migrants seeking admission to the United States are now being sent back to Mexico for the duration of their court proceedings. They are allowed to cross the border only for their hearings, often conducted in an expanding network of tent courts.

The migrants' chances of gaining entry into the United States were further impaired last month when the Supreme Court let stand another new Trump administration policy that requires migrants who traveled through other countries en route to the United States to prove they had been denied asylum along the way before being eligible to apply at the border.

More than 50,000 migrants have been sent back from various southern border entry points, including about 120 a day who are being returned to Matamoros.

Not only has the plaza encampment near the bridge in Matamoros grown more crowded by the day, say volunteers who have worked with the group, but in a town that is notorious for drug and gang violence, some migrants have been victims of kidnapping for extortion and sexual assault.

Thursday's protest at the bridge was peaceful, witnesses said. By early afternoon about 150 migrants remained, despite reminders by the authorities that the protocols for admission would not be waived. After a visit by immigrant advocates and the mayor of Matamoros, they dispersed in the late afternoon and the lanes reopened to traffic.

The Gateway bridge closure had caused long lines to form at two other international bridges leading into Texas, and border officials said Thursday's scheduled immigration court hearings in Brownsville were postponed.

Emigdio Manuel García, 89, who owns a restaurant and curios shop in Matamoros about a block from the bridge, expressed exasperation over the disruption caused by the closure. "These people have been here for many months," he said. "They are now invading the international bridge to protest and they are blocking passage."

Mr. Garcia said the bridge was vital to the economy of both cities. The shutdown, he said, affects "people who are trying to get their kids to school, who are trying to go shopping."

"Matamoros and Brownsville are one single city, a city joined by a bridge that is now dividing us," he added.

There have been attempts by migrants to rush two other international bridges in South Texas in recent months. In June and July, authorities at the Hidalgo-Reynosa International Bridge intercepted a handful of migrants trying to run across. Several migrants also attempted to get across the bridge connecting Reynosa, Mexico, and Pharr, Texas.

In November last year, a peaceful march by Central American migrants waiting in Mexico across from California veered out of control as hundreds tried to evade a Mexican police blockade and run toward the border crossing into San Diego.

In response, the American authorities shut down the border crossing in both directions and fired tear gas to repel migrants, most of whom had been traveling as part of a large caravan.

MITCHELL FERMAN and **ELDA CANTÚ** contributed reporting.

Glossary

affidavit A written statement confirmed by oath that can be used as evidence in legal proceedings.

asylum seeker A person who has left their home country as a political refugee and is now seeking protection.

autonomy The ability to determine actions independently or to self-rule.

cartel An association of manufacturers bound together in order to restrict competition. Often used in reference to drug cartels, which are criminal organizations unifying drug trafficking operations.

dehumanization The process of stripping away an individual's human qualities and dignity.

deportation The forced expulsion of an individual from a country.

detention The act of forcibly keeping an individual in official custody.

enclave A place that is different in character from its surrounding environment.

fraudulent Obtained or achieved by deception or other false means.

ICE Immigration and Customs Enforcement, or the federal law enforcement agency that controls U.S. border policy.

impetus A force or event that makes an action or activity happen more quickly.

myriad Extremely large in number.

persecution Cruel or hostile treatment over a significant period of time based on race, political or religious beliefs, or social factors.

petition A formal request appealing to authority to undertake an action.

prototypical Indicating the first or the most usual form of something.

provisional Temporary; arranged for the present, possibly to be changed later.

post-traumatic stress disorder (PTSD) A mental health condition triggered by a shocking, frightening or traumatic event.

refoulement The forcible return of refugees or asylum seekers to a country where they are at risk of being subjected to continued persecution.

refugee An individual forced to leave their country in order to escape war, persecution or natural disaster. Refugees differ from asylum seekers in that asylum seekers are already in the country when they make their claim.

retribution Punishment inflicted on someone as vengeance.

sanctuary city A city whose local laws seek to protect undocumented immigrants from deportation or persecution.

xenophobia Dislike of or prejudice against people from other countries.

Media Literacy Terms

"Media literacy" refers to the ability to access, understand, critically assess and create media. The following terms are important components of media literacy, and they will help you critically engage with the articles in this title.

angle The aspect of a news story that a journalist focuses on and develops.

attribution The method by which a source is identified or by which facts and information are assigned to the person who provided them.

balance Principle of journalism that both perspectives of an argument should be presented in a fair way.

bias A disposition of prejudice in favor of a certain idea, person or perspective.

chronological order Method of writing a story presenting the details of the story in the order in which they occurred.

column A type of story that is a regular feature, often on a recurring topic, written by the same journalist, generally known as a columnist.

commentary A type of story that is an expression of opinion on recent events by a journalist generally known as a commentator.

credibility The quality of being trustworthy and believable, said of a journalistic source.

editorial Article of opinion or interpretation.

fake news A fictional or made-up story presented in the style of a legitimate news story, intended to deceive readers; also commonly used to criticize legitimate news that one dislikes because of its perspective or unfavorable coverage of a subject.

human interest story A type of story that focuses on individuals and how events or issues affect their life, generally offering a sense of relatability to the reader.

impartiality Principle of journalism that a story should not reflect a journalist's bias and should contain balance.

intention The motive or reason behind something, such as the publication of a news story.

news story An article or style of expository writing that reports news, generally in a straightforward fashion and without editorial comment.

op-ed An opinion piece that reflects a prominent individual's opinion on a topic of interest.

paraphrase The summary of an individual's words, with attribution, rather than a direct quotation of their exact words.

plagiarism An attempt to pass another person's work as one's own without attribution.

quotation The use of an individual's exact words indicated by the use of quotation marks and proper attribution.

reliability The quality of being dependable and accurate, said of a journalistic source.

rhetorical device Technique in writing intending to persuade the reader or communicate a message from a certain perspective.

source The origin of the information reported in journalism.

style A distinctive use of language in writing or speech; also a news or publishing organization's rules for consistent use of language with regards to spelling, punctuation, typography and capitalization, usually regimented by a house style guide.

tone A manner of expression in writing or speech.

Media Literacy Questions

1. Identify the various sources cited in the article "Inside an Immigrant Caravan: Women and Children, Fleeing Violence" (on page 150). How does Kirk Semple attribute information to each of these sources in his article? How effective are Semple's attributions in helping the reader identify his sources?

2. In "With Trump's Tough Deterrents, Many Asylum Seekers on the Border are Giving Up" (on page 118), Jose A. Del Real, Caitlin Dickerson and Miriam Jordan paraphrase information from Natali. What are the strengths of the use of a paraphrase as opposed to a direct quote? What are the weaknesses?

3. Compare the headlines of "Waiting for Asylum in the United States, Migrants Live in Fear in Mexico" (on page 124) and " 'Every Day I Fear': Asylum Seekers Await Their Fate in a Clogged System" (on page 135). Which is a more compelling headline, and why? How could the less compelling headline be changed to better draw the reader's interest?

4. Does Patrick Kingsley demonstrate the journalistic principle of impartiality in his article "Is Trump's America Tougher on Asylum Than Other Western Countries?" (on page 42)? If so, how did he do so? If not, what could Kingsley have included to make his article more impartial?

5. Does " 'This Takes Away All Hope': Rule Bars Most Applicants for Asylum in U.S." (on page 78) use multiple sources? What are the strengths of using multiple sources in a journalistic piece? What are the weaknesses of relying heavily on only one or a few sources?

6. "Waiting for Asylum in the United States, Migrants Live in Fear in Mexico" (on page 124) features photographs. What do these photographs add to the article?

7. What is the intention of the article "Who Qualifies for 'Asylum'?" (on page 23)? How effectively does it achieve its intended purpose?

8. Analyze the authors' reporting in "Most Migrants at Border With Mexico Would Be Denied Asylum Protections Under New Trump Rule" (on page 67) and "On the Border, a Discouraging New Message for Asylum Seekers: Wait" (on page 109). Do you think one article is more balanced in its reporting than the other? If so, why do you think so?

9. Identify each of the sources in "Women Are Fleeing Death at Home. The U.S. Wants to Keep Them Out." (on page 172) as a primary source or a secondary source. Evaluate the reliability and credibility of each source. How does your evaluation of each source change your perspective on this article?

10. What type of story is "Trump Is Trying to Kill the Program That Saved My Life" (on page 206)? Can you identify another article in this collection that is the same type of story? What elements helped you come to your conclusion?

Citations

All citations in this list are formatted according to the Modern Language Association's (MLA) style guide.

BOOK CITATION

THE NEW YORK TIMES EDITORIAL STAFF. *Seeking Asylum: The Human Cost.* New York Times Educational Publishing, 2021.

ONLINE ARTICLE CITATIONS

AHMED, AZAM. "Women Are Fleeing Death at Home. The U.S. Wants to Keep Them Out." *The New York Times*, 18 Aug. 2019, https://www.nytimes.com /2019/08/18/world/americas/guatemala-violence-women-asylum.html.

AHMED, AZAM, AND PAULINA VILLEGAS. " 'This Takes Away All Hope': Rule Bars Most Applicants for Asylum in U.S." *The New York Times*, 12 Sept. 2019, https://www.nytimes.com/2019/09/12/world/americas/Asylum-seekers.html.

BAZELON, EMILY. "Who Qualifies for 'Asylum'?" *The New York Times,* 15 Sept. 2015, https://www.nytimes.com/2015/09/20/magazine/who -qualifies-for-asylum.html.

BENNER, KATIE, AND CAITLIN DICKERSON. "Sessions Says Domestic and Gang Violence Are Not Grounds for Asylum." *The New York Times*, 11 June 2018, https://www.nytimes.com/2018/06/11/us/politics/sessions-domestic -violence-asylum.html.

BILEFSKY, DAN. "Gays Seeking Asylum in U.S. Encounter a New Hurdle." *The New York Times*, 28 Jan. 2011, https://www.nytimes.com/2011/01/29 /nyregion/29asylum.html.

CANTÚ, FRANCISCO. "Seeking Refuge, Legally, and Finding Prison." *The New York Times*, 31 May 2019, https://www.nytimes.com/2019/05/31/opinion /power-asylum-seekers.html.

DEL REAL, JOSE A., ET AL. "With Trump's Tough Deterrents, Many Asylum Seekers on the Border Are Giving Up." *The New York Times*, 16 Feb. 2019,

https://www.nytimes.com/2019/02/16/us/border-migrants-asylum
-mexico-aclu.html.

DICKERSON, CAITLIN, AND MIRIAM JORDAN. " 'No Asylum Here': Some Say U.S.
Border Agents Rejected Them." *The New York Times*, 3 May 2017, https://
www.nytimes.com/2017/05/03/us/asylum-border-customs.html.

FERNANDEZ, MANNY. "A New Migrant Surge at the Border, This One From
Central Africa." *The New York Times*, 16 June 2019, https://www.nytimes
.com/2019/06/16/us/border-africans-congo-maine.html.

GOLDBAUM, CHRISTINA. " 'I Don't Want to Die': Asylum Seekers, Once in Limbo,
Face Deportation Under Trump." *The New York Times*, 21 Apr. 2019, https://
www.nytimes.com/2019/04/21/nyregion/asylum-seekers-deportation.html.

HABERMAN, CLYDE. "Trump and the Battle Over Sanctuary in America."
The New York Times, 5 Mar. 2017, https://www.nytimes.com/2017/03/05
/us/sanctuary-cities-movement-1980s-political-asylum.html.

JORDAN, MIRIAM. "Asylum Protesters Close Bridge on Texas-Mexico Border."
The New York Times, 10 Oct. 2019, https://www.nytimes.com/2019/10/10
/us/brownsville-texas-border-protest.html.

JORDAN, MIRIAM. "A Refugee Caravan Is Hoping for Asylum in the U.S. How
Are These Cases Decided?" *The New York Times*, 30 Apr. 2018, https://
www.nytimes.com/2018/04/30/us/migrant-caravan-asylum.html.

JORDAN, MIRIAM, AND JOSE A. DEL REAL. " 'Every Day I Fear': Asylum
Seekers Await Their Fate in a Clogged System." *The New York Times*,
1 May 2019, https://www.nytimes.com/2019/05/01/us/asylum-seekers
-trump-memo.html.

JORDAN, MIRIAM, AND SIMON ROMERO. "What It Takes to Get Asylum in the
U.S." *The New York Times*, 2 May 2018, https://www.nytimes.com/2018
/05/02/us/what-it-takes-to-get-asylum-us.html.

KANNO-YOUNGS, ZOLAN, AND MAYA AVERBUCH. "Waiting for Asylum in the
United States, Migrants Live in Fear in Mexico." *The New York Times*,
5 Apr. 2019, https://www.nytimes.com/2019/04/05/us/politics/asylum
-united-states-migrants-mexico.html.

KANNO-YOUNGS, ZOLAN, AND MIRIAM JORDAN. "New Trump Administration
Proposal Would Charge Asylum Seekers an Application Fee." *The New
York Times*, 8 Nov. 2019, https://www.nytimes.com/2019/11/08/us/politics
/immigration-fees-trump.html.

KANNO-YOUNGS, ZOLAN, AND ELISABETH MALKIN. "U.S. Agreement With El
Salvador Seeks to Divert Asylum Seekers." *The New York Times*, 20 Sept.

2019, https://www.nytimes.com/2019/09/20/us/politics/us-asylum-el
-salvador.html.

KINGSLEY, PATRICK. "Is Trump's America Tougher on Asylum Than Other
Western Countries?" *The New York Times*, 14 Sept. 2019, https://www
.nytimes.com/2019/09/14/world/europe/trump-america-asylum-migration
.html.

KOTHOR, MARIUS. "Trump Is Trying to Kill the Program That Saved My Life."
The New York Times, 2 Oct. 2019, https://www.nytimes.com/2019/10/02
/opinion/trump-refugee-program.html.

LELAND, JOHN. "Fleeing Violence in Honduras, a Teenage Boy Seeks Asylum
in Brooklyn." *The New York Times*, 5 Dec. 2014, https://www.nytimes
.com/2014/12/07/nyregion/fleeing-violence-in-honduras-a-teenage-boy
-seeks-asylum-in-brooklyn.html.

LEUTERT, STEPHANIE, AND SHAW DRAKE. " 'We Are Full': What Asylum
Seekers Are Told." *The New York Times*, 28 Jan. 2019, https://www.nytimes
.com/2019/01/28/opinion/asylum-border-immigrants-trump-.html.

NAZARIO, SONIA. " 'Someone Is Always Trying to Kill You.' " *The New York
Times*, 5 Apr. 2019, https://www.nytimes.com/interactive/2019/04/05
/opinion/honduras-women-murders.html.

THE NEW YORK TIMES. "Children Shouldn't Be Dying at the Border. Here's
How You Can Help." *The New York Times*, 24 June 2019, https://www
.nytimes.com/2019/06/24/opinion/border-kids-immigration-help.html.

PRESTON, JULIA. "Big Disparities in Judging of Asylum Cases." *The New
York Times*, 31 May 2007, https://www.nytimes.com/2007/05/31
/washington/31asylum.html.

PRESTON, JULIA. "Losing Asylum, Then His Life." *The New York Times*,
28 June 2010, https://www.nytimes.com/2010/06/29/us/29asylum.html.

PRESTON, JULIA. "New Policy Permits Asylum for Battered Women." *The
New York Times*, 15 July, 2009, https://www.nytimes.com/2009/07/16
/us/16asylum.html.

ROMERO, SIMON, AND MIRIAM JORDAN. "On the Border, a Discouraging New
Message for Asylum Seekers: Wait." *The New York Times*, 12 June 2018,
https://www.nytimes.com/2018/06/12/us/asylum-seekers-mexico-border
.html.

RUBIN, ELIZABETH. "Locked Up for Seeking Asylum." *The New York Times*,
2 Apr. 2016, https://www.nytimes.com/2016/04/03/opinion/sunday/locked
-up-for-seeking-asylum.html.

SEMPLE, KIRK. "Inside an Immigrant Caravan: Women and Children, Fleeing Violence." *The New York Times*, 4 Apr. 2018, https://www.nytimes.com /2018/04/04/world/americas/mexico-trump-caravan.html.

SEMPLE, KIRK. "The U.S. and Guatemala Reached an Asylum Deal: Here's What It Means." *The New York Times*, 28 July 2019, https://www.nytimes .com/2019/07/28/world/americas/guatemala-safe-third-asylum.html.

SHEAR, MICHAEL D., AND ZOLAN KANNO-YOUNGS. "Most Migrants at Border With Mexico Would Be Denied Asylum Protections Under New Trump Rule." *The New York Times*, 15 July 2019, https://www.nytimes.com/2019 /07/15/us/politics/trump-asylum-rule.html.

SHEAR, MICHAEL D., AND ZOLAN KANNO-YOUNGS. "Trump Administration to Push for Tougher Asylum Rules." *The New York Times*, 9 Apr. 2019, https://www.nytimes.com/2019/04/09/us/politics/asylum-seekers-trump -administration.html.

SHEAR, MICHAL D., ET AL. "What Will Trump's Tough New Asylum Policy Mean for Migrants on the Border?" *The New York Times*, 17 Apr. 2019, https://www.nytimes.com/2019/04/17/us/politics/asylum-facts-seekers -laws.html.

SURO, ROBERTO. "We Need to Offer More Than Asylum." *The New York Times*, 14 July 2018, https://www.nytimes.com/2018/07/14/opinion/sunday /migration-asylum-trump.html.

TACKETT, MICHAEL, ET AL. "Migrants Seeking Asylum Must Wait in Mexico, Trump Administration Says." *The New York Times*, 20 Dec. 2018, https:// www.nytimes.com/2018/12/20/us/politics/mexico-trump-asylum-seekers -migrants.html.

VERHOVEK, SAM HOWE. "In a Shift, U.S. Grants Asylum for Mexicans." *The New York Times*, 1 Dec. 1995, https://www.nytimes.com/1995/12/01 /us/in-a-shift-us-grants-asylum-for-mexicans.html.

ZAVERI, MIHIR. "Asylum Officers' Union Says Trump Migration Policy 'Abandons' American Tradition." *The New York Times*, 26 June 2019, https://www.nytimes.com/2019/06/26/us/asylum-officers-trump -migrants.html.

Index

This book is current up until the time of printing. For the most up-to-date reporting, visit www.nytimes.com.